Confessions Of A First Lady 3

BY

Denora M. Boone

Acknowledgements

First and foremost I have to give all of the honor to my Lord and Savior. It is through Him that I am living a dream that I never knew I would have but I am so thankful that He blessed me with it.

My husband Byron and our children will always be my biggest supporters and I can't thank them enough for helping me on this journey. Nights like tonight Byron has stayed up just to keep me company knowing that he had to go to work the next day. Baby your sacrifice does not go unnoticed and I thank you so much!

    My publisher David Weaver thank you for just continuing to let God express Himself through me for His people. I know it's tough dealing with me and the way that I have to write in order to make it the best but you never say anything negative even if I know you may want to. Lol

    To my Anointed Inspirations Family I try my best to go so hard for you all because you go hard for me. I love yall and thank you for understanding that not only am I a publisher but an author as well and some days I just have to close myself away to get things done. It makes it so much easier to have a team like that standing with me.

To my readers...you are who I do this for and yall have been so patient while I work on different projects. I know this one was looooooong overdue but here it is! I pray that it blesses you and that all questions are answered and Pastor nem'

can finally rest. Enjoy!

Previously……

Marcus

It was show time.

"Marcus get the doctor. I have to push!" Veronica said handing my little Cadence to her mother but not before giving her another kiss on her fat cheek.

Everyone left the room as the doctor rushed in dressed for the occasion.

"Mr. Millhouse you might want to put this on as fast as you can so you don't mess up your clothes." He said as the nurse handed me a set of scrubs.

"Please hold on until I change baby. I have never missed any of our kids being born and I don't plan on doing it now." I said as I kissed her.

"I know that and you know that but our baby has no idea. He's ready to meet the man he's heard about for the last few months." She replied smiling.

I ran off into the bathroom and knew I didn't have enough time to fully change so I just pulled the uniform over my own clothes and hurried out.

"Alright Veronica with this next contraction I want you to push as hard as you can." Dr. Warren instructed her.

I made the mistake once again of giving her my hand to hold. During each labor I had given her my hand to hold and she brought me to tears. My wife wasn't the smallest woman and she was by far the biggest but the strength she had in the time of pain baffled me. I couldn't let go even if I wanted to.

Forty five minutes and many pushes later God allowed our youngest son Christian Immanuel Millhouse to enter the world.

"I can't believe we just had another baby." I said as I held our son close to my heart.

"Are you ok with it? I mean I know that we didn't plan this." Veronica asked me.

"Our ways are not like God's ways and our thoughts are not His. But in the end they all work out for our good and I'm so grateful to him that he has blessed us with this gift and bringing you back to us unharmed." I said to her as I sat on the bed and kissed her as deeply as I could. I wanted her to feel the deepest part of my soul and know that now that I had her back I was never letting her go.

"Uh isn't that how you got this baby?" we heard Destiny say as she and her sister cracked up.

"I would tell you to get you some bizniee but because I'm in such a happy place I'm gonna let that comment slide this time." I said laughing along with them. I finally had my whole family back and nothing was going to take that away from me.

If there is one thing I learned throughout life when you experience the good be prepared for the ugly head of the enemy to try and throw a monkey wrench in the mix. Of course I knew that something would rear its ugly head sooner or later. I just hoped it was the later. But with the way things had been set up in my life these days I knew trouble was about to hit.

 Just as I was about to say a prayer for our family there was a knock at the door. Everyone was already in the room including the doctor so I had no idea who it could have been. Malachi was the closest to the door and the look on his face after he opened it confirmed that some more mess was getting ready to hit the fan.

He slowly moved away from the door and entered Veronica's mother Sarita. I had been so focused on getting here as fast as I could from Atlanta that it never crossed my mind to find out where Sarita or Iesha's parents had gone. I just knew I had to get to my wife.

The closer she got to the bed it seemed like everyone had been holding their breaths because none of us knew how this reunion would go. I looked at Veronica and saw that once the recognition flashed across her face things were about to go left real quick.

Veronica didn't even have the chance to utter a word before her mother spoke.

"Veronica I apologize for everything that happened in your life. I now know how my actions hurt you even though I thought I was protecting you. I never knew that your father would hurt you so much and I don't think I will ever forgive myself for this pain. But I pray that you can find it in your heart to forgive me. I not only caused you harm but your sister as well. I want the two of you to eventually find a common ground before I leave this earth. I want to know that my girls are in each other's lives the way it should have been from the beginning." Sarita poured out all of her emotions during this plea.

I don't think anyone was breathing and when Veronica finally spoke for the first time I knew everybody in there had to have died because I was definitely having an out of body experience.

"I can forgive you mother." She said sounding so cold that the hair on the back of my neck stood at attention and my arms filled with goose bumps.

"Thank you baby." Sarita said not picking up on the same thing that I did. Something was terribly wrong.

"But what I won't do is forgive your trifling daughter. Adrian is it? It's one thing to drug my husband and then seduce him but it is something totally different when she doesn't even consider using a condom to prevent herself from getting pregnant by him. She should be going into labor any day now right Mommy Dearest?" she ended causing my world to stop yet again.

Chapter One

Three Months Ago……

Veronica

I thought back to the time that I spent away from my family. It had been a miracle that I had delivered a healthy baby boy knowing everything that my body had gone through. Some days there were beatings and others there was no food. Keith would switch it up on me all depending on how he felt that day and if he had talked to Adrian or not.

    I figured this out by pretending I was asleep when he would be on the phone. If he was quiet and laughed periodically I knew that the conversation was going well and I would be treated kindly. Then there were the times when he didn't get a call all day and he would start to panic or the conversation wasn't going as he had hoped. That would be when things got ugly.

For a while I prayed that he received the good calls but when the bad ones came more frequently I just prayed that my baby and I would survive and we had. The moment I was finally able to hold him in my arms and see the look of joy on the faces of Marcus and our children I knew that God was still there. Then He left and hasn't returned since.

When my mother came to the hospital after I delivered Christian, part of me wanted her to hold me and tell me that everything was all a dream. Then there was the part of me who wanted nothing to do with her at all. I still couldn't understand how a mother just walked away from her child without a second thought. Then something came over me and I wanted to forgive her. Or maybe I needed to forgive her. Whatever was causing me to do it I knew once I did that heaviness would no longer hold me down.

    Now forgiving the woman who I had just found out to be my sister would be the challenge. I didn't even know her like that but I hated her so much it hurt. I knew everyone was confused as to how I had known that Adrian was my sister and pregnant by my husband but Keith had shared that bit of information with me already. I could tell that he didn't want to tell me but his hand was forced which made it easier for Adrian to be on my hit list.

On one of the rare instances Keith had gone out and come back to the house with take out. Immediately my stomach growled and my mouth watered just praying that he had some for me. Usually he made me eat only a cheese sandwich and a half of glass of water but today he came in with two boxes of food and two large strawberry lemonades. All the angels in heaven knew I needed a good meal.

    I watched as he brought a chair into the bedroom and sat down opening one of the carry out trays. I knew from the look of it he had gone to Mr. Everything Café. That gave me confirmation that I was at least still in Georgia but didn't know where. We could be down the street from the café or over thirty minutes away but at least I was in my home state. The smell of the food hit my nose again. Jesus take me now because this was about to kill me if I didn't at least get a spoonful.

"You want some huh?" Keith teased knowing good and well what my answer was.

Reaching down to the floor he picked up the other plate and drink and brought it over to me. He would strap me down to the bed whenever he left so that I wouldn't try and find a way out so I was still tied by my feet to the bed post. I almost dropped it trying to get to the food so fast and when I finally got it opened I wanted to cry. Looking back at me was a hearty helping of shrimp, steak, chicken, cheese, broccoli, and spinach over some yellow rice. God is good!

It took me under ten minutes to finish the whole thing and while I was drinking he spoke again. This time his face held a smirk that was unsettling. I thought maybe he put something in my food.

"You know your sister was right about you. You don't care anything about her." He said throwing me for a loop.

"What are you talking about?" I asked him?

"I hear you in here praying all day and all night for everyone but her. Why is that?"

"What sister? I'm an only child I don't have a sister." I said confused.

For a split second he looked as if he was contemplating if I was telling the truth or not. It was hard to read Keith most of the time and I guess that was how the police academy trained them.

"Adrian said that you would act like this. I figured she was just exaggerating but I guess she knew what she was talking about." He said getting up.

The name Adrian sounded so familiar but I didn't know where I had heard it from then it dawned on me.

"Wait Officer Norman? She was the one who was at the scene of the accident I had first." I said stunned. Why was she saying that she was my sister when I had just met her that day?

"Oh now you know her huh?"

"Only because I remembered her name but how do you figure that's my sister?" None of this was making sense and I was tired of Keith playing with me.

"Just tell me what you're talking about!" I yelled. I was getting so worked up that I was getting nauseous and needed to vomit. The food wasn't agreeing with me or baby right now.

Walking back over to the bed he looked down into my face. I felt like all of my energy was draining out of me and my eyelids were getting heavy.

"I'll leave that up to her to explain the details but I do have one more question." He said just as my eyes were about to close. It was then that I knew he had put something in either the lemonade or my food.

I couldn't respond or even nod my head to let him know that something was wrong so I just laid there.

"How does it feel to know that your sister is having your husband's baby too?"

I didn't remember anything after that and when I woke up I felt like I had been asleep for weeks. It wasn't until I was finally free and in labor and saw my mother walk into the delivery room that all of those memories came back flooding my memory.

That's the reason they looked at me the way they did when I blurted out that I knew Adrian was pregnant. I was praying that Marcus didn't know what I was talking about. That would let me know that maybe Keith was just trying to get me upset but when I saw the look on Marcus' face I knew that it was true. The man that I had loved for what seemed like forever had gotten my long lost sister pregnant.

The buck didn't stop there though. I still hadn't come to terms with all of these revelations from my ex-lover trying to rekindle an old flame that had been put out long ago, to my long lost mother and sister showing up. Then to be told that this was all a plot to come at me for just moving on with my life made it worse. The day Mother Johnson called me it felt like the hell on earth I was living in had just gotten hotter.

Three days after I had come home from the hospital Marcus received a phone call late one night. It was about eight thirty at night and we were in bed admiring our newest addition to the family. The girl's had gone to bed and MJ was in his room with

Cadence and talking on the phone to Lailani. I couldn't have been prouder of my son than I was right now for him stepping up to his responsibilities.

"Hello?" Marcus answered his cell phone.

I watched as he eased out of the bed and walked over to the dresser to get his keys and wallet out of his top drawer. He looked up and noticed the questioning look on my face and lifted his index finger to let me know to hold on a second.

"Umm ok then. I'm on my way. No she's in bed with Christian. Ok I'm on the way." He said hanging up. Now I needed to know who he was talking to and why they were concerned about where I was. Call it what you want but I knew something was wrong and he was not telling me.

"So where are you going? It's not late but still." I said with a little more attitude than I intended. These hormones of mine were still trippin'.

"I just need to go and check on, um one of the members at the hospital. I won't be gone long and I'll call you when I'm on my way home." He said kissing me and rushing out before I could object.

I said a quick prayer for him and got back to spending time with my newborn. I loved everything about him from his beautiful dark brown eyes to his curly hair that was already long enough to put in a ponytail. He looked just like the perfect mixture of Marcus and I. I watched as his little chest rose up and down and he smiled occasionally in his sleep. Marcus had been gone about forty five minutes and I was just about to try and catch a quick nap just as my cell phone rang.

I looked down and frowned wondering why Mother Johnson was calling me so late.

"Hey Mama are you ok?" I asked alarmed. I knew that she lived with her daughter Ashley who was also a member of our church but she worked nights as an RN at the hospital.

"I was calling to ask you the same thing baby. I know you just had little man and were recovering from your ordeal. Ashley just slipped away to call me to let me know she just saw Pastor rushing up to labor and delivery. She thought something was wrong with you again but she didn't have time to go and ask." She said confusing me.

"Well I'm at home mama. Is Ash sure that it was Marcus?" I asked trying to give him the benefit of the doubt.

"Oh yes. She said what made her notice him was because an older lady that looked a lot like you called his name to show him where to come. Ashley was on the elevator with a patient and just as the door closed she heard him call her Sarita."

It took every fiber of my being and every angel in heaven to keep me from blowing up while on the phone with this woman. I couldn't believe after all of these years with Marcus that he just flat out lied to me about where he was going and who had called him. Especially knowing the bad blood that was still lingering. I knew when Mother Johnson said that he was on the Labor and Delivery floor and my mother was there, the person he was going to see was Adrian.

"Oh yes. I feel asleep and forgot that he was going up to visit one of our family members at the hospital. This little guy has my mind all mixed up these days." I chuckled but there was no humor to be found in it. Mother Johnson picked up on it but didn't say anything about it.

"Well ok then baby. You get some rest. I'm glad that you are all ok."

"Thank you so much for checking on us. I'll see you all in a few weeks at church."

"I can't wait to see you. And Veronica?" she said calling me by my first name. I knew that she was serious when she did that.

"Ma'am?"

"Everything may not always be as it seems. Keep listening for the voice of the

Lord and He will give you clarity ok?" she said before ending the call.

I took heed to Mother Johnson's warning just a little bit so before I jumped in my car I placed a call to Marcus' phone. It rang twice before he sent me to voicemail. Now I for one was usually calm and demure in a lot of situations but he was about to see a side of me that he wasn't ready for. I tried calling two more times back to back and he sent me to voicemail until he finally turned his phone off.

"Oh he trying it! You want to see if I'm really bout that life huh?" I said out loud as I got up and threw on my red sweats with the matching hoodie and my red and black Jordan 13's. I picked up Christian along with his pacifier and blanket and headed to MJ's room.

I knocked on his door and didn't bother to wait until he answered as I walked right in. He had Cadence in her crib asleep as he lay across his bed watching a movie.

"Hey young thugga where you going?" He asked me as he laughed but quickly stopped when he noticed I wasn't in the mood.

"I need you to watch your brother for a few minutes. I have to run to the hospital with your father right quick." I said as he took the baby from me while he continued to stare me down.

"You know I got you but Ma what's going on? You don't look like yourself." My son said concerned. As much as I wanted to let him know wat was going on with me I had to remind myself he was still my child and he didn't need to carry my burdens along with his.

"Honestly I haven't been myself in quite some time but I will be ok. His milk is in the fridge and you know where the pampers are. I will have my phone on and I shouldn't be gone no longer than an hour. Call me if you need me and I'll come right back." I said running down my instructions to MJ. He simply nodded his head as he put the baby on his chest and laid back on his bed. I smiled at the sight before leaving but not missing the look of worry on my oldest child's face.

Heading to the garage with my keys in hand and my id in my pocket I turned on the alarm and hopped into my car. I didn't want to get pulled over without my license on me but I wasn't trying to carry a purse on this mission. The less I had to carry the better.

Backing out of the driveway I caught a glimpse of myself in the mirror and the person looking back at me I almost didn't recognize. Well it wasn't that I didn't recognize her I just hadn't seen her in a long time. I looked at the person staring back at me and knew that if God was still with me then He was going to have to meet me at this hospital because if He didn't it was about to be a situation.

MJ must have been driving my car because his music started playing when I hit the power button to the CD player. Some song came on called 'Love Don't Change' by somebody named Jeremih. I don't know what God was trying to tell me through this song but something in me broke when I heard him say, when it hurts, I can make it better. Girl if it works, it's gon' be forever. We been through the worst, made it through the weather. Our problems and the pain but love don't change.

God knows I didn't want the love I shared with Marcus to change but as I drove and the closer I got to the hospital I wasn't sure anymore. Depending on what I found when I got inside would determine if our love indeed had changed.

I parked and walked in through the emergency room entrance since the main door to the hospital was now locked. Walking over to the triage station I put a big phony smile on my face. After I got off of the phone with Mother Johnson I figured that Adrian had gone into labor and my mother had been the one to call and let Marcus know.

"Hi can I help you?" said the nurse asked. I read the name on her badge and it said Melissa.

"Yes Melissa. My sister is here having her first baby and my mother called but I was so excited that I forgot to ask what room she was in." I chuckled as I lied clean through my teeth. I probably should have repented for that lie but I was just gonna wait until I got upstairs cause the way my mood was set up I knew I was going to have more that I needed to add on.

"How exciting! Let me see if I can find her. What's your sister's name?" Melissa asked just a little too bubbly for me. I had to fight the urge to roll my eyes until she looked away.

"Her name is Adrian Norman." I told her crossing my arms across my chest so that she couldn't see my hands shaking.

It was taking her a little too long to get the information pulled up and I started second guessing if I was wrong or not. Just as I was about to tell her maybe I had the wrong hospital she began to speak.

"Yes I found her. I see that she has a visitor's list already set up and you're already on it. She is in room 3255." She smiled at me.

  Buzzing me into the back and giving me the directions to get to the room I thanked her and found the elevator that I needed. As soon as I got on and the doors closed I started to hyperventilate. How in the world was I on a list that I knew nothing about? Nothing was making sense and I needed to get it together before I found her room.

My breathing finally became steady just as the doors opened and I stepped off. The smell of saline, machines beeping, and faint baby cries consumed me. Out of nowhere I began to feel nauseous when I stepped in front of room 3255 and realized the cries I heard from the elevator were coming from behind this door.

I pushed the door open as Marcus turned around holding a crying bundle with a smile so big on his face. That was until he noticed it was me and the smile became nonexistent. I looked over at my so called mother on the telephone looking like a deer caught in headlights and right before anyone could speak the bathroom door opened and out comes Adrian wearing a smirk on her face.

All I saw was red and it was go time!

Chapter Two

Sarita

      Oh my God this was not the way this was supposed to be happening right now. I called Marcus so that I could let both him and Veronica know that Adrian was in labor and wanted the both of them to be there. I had finally talked her into trying to make things work and repair the relationship between her and her sister. Adrian said that she was more than ready and that she wanted her sister in her life so when Marcus showed up here alone I was confused. I knew that Veronica had a newborn at home but I requested that they both come together. The last thing I wanted was for anything else to draw a wedge between them.

When I came to the hospital the day Veronica was found that was the first time I had seen her since she was seven years old. I knew when she said that she had forgiven me but not her sister it was going to take a lot to mend this. What shocked me though was how she knew that Adrian was pregnant and by Marcus at that. Even I was shocked by that. The reason I had called Marcus' phone tonight was because Veronica had somehow blocked my number so he was my only option.

"YOU NO GOOD HOMEWRECKER!" Was all I heard before Veronica was on Adrian like white on rice.

In all honesty though I really couldn't blame her for responding the way she was right now. She had been through so much recently and to walk in to find her husband holding what was possibly a child he made with her sister and her mother in the room too made her snap.

It made me think about the time Shonda Briscoe tried me about Clarence and I went off. Veronica was definitely my child. Now had this been any other time and place I may have let Veronica get all of her aggression out but we were in the hospital and there was a newborn in the room so I had to get the situation under control as fast as I could.

Veronica was definitely my daughter because she was as strong as an ox!

"SEE. YOU. THOUGHT. I. WAS. SOMEBODY. TO. PLAY. WITH. BUT. I DON'T PLAY. WITH. OTHER. FOLKS. KIDS!" Veronica said with every punch she landed. Adrian was trying her best to swing back and actually landed a punch but that just made Veronica go in harder.

"OH! YOU. WANT. TO. FIGHT. BACK? YOU OLE NO GOOD. LOW LIFE. UNHAPPY. VAGINA SLANGING. VERONICA MILLHOUSE

WANNA BE! YOU WANT MY LIFE HUH? YOU WANT TO BE ME THAT BAD THAT YOU HAVE TO TRICK MY HUSBAND INTO SLEEPING WITH YOU?" Veronica ranted.

Marcus had finally gotten a hold of his wife and I was wondering where the nurses or doctors were because no one had rushed in. I know they had to have heard the commotion and we needed some help in here. I did my best to hold onto Adrian but my grip was slipping. She was some kind of strong too but not a match for her sister.

"Nobody had to trick him! It wasn't that much that I put into his water so he knew what was going on. He liked it! Didn't you baby?" Adrian teased.

I looked at Adrian and didn't know who it was that I was looking at. This wasn't the child that I'd raised and I started second guessing myself for even calling Marcus. Had I known this was going to happen I would have just waited. While I was contemplating on my next move to resolve this I didn't see when Marcus caught an elbow to his ribs from Veronica and she broke free. That split second mess up gave Veronica just enough time to get back on top of Adrian and begin beating her some more.

Veronica had Adrian by her throat with her nails digging into her throat as she spoke with so much venom that I didn't recognize her voice.

"You better hope you die because if you don't and I ever see you again I will forget that I'm saved and I will gut you like a fish. As much pain as I'm harboring because of you, Iesha, and your little do boy Keith I will plead insanity and do my time proudly. Now try me if you want to." She said letting go of Adrian's neck as she fell to the floor.

The door opened and I was praying that someone was coming to help instead it was her friend Torre followed by her husband Malachi and two nurses.

"Sis? Come on V let's go mama. I got you boo, come on the kids need you." Torrie said trying to touch Veronica's shoulder as she snatched away ad walked over to Marcus.

Looking at the baby who was now laying quietly in the bassinet she rolled her eyes looking disgusted and focused back on her husband. She was so close to him I knew that he could feel the heat radiating off of her body.

"If you know like I know you better beat me home." Was all that she said before she turned and walked out of the door.

All I could do was look at Adrian who was still trying to catch her breath and shake my head. Over the years I had built a good relationship with God and I knew that no one could fix this but Him. I just prayed it was in His will to bring my family back together.

Chapter Three

Marcus

    I couldn't believe this was happening but what I did know was that I better make it home before my wife did. When I got the call from Sarita I thought it would be best that I handled the situation myself without involving Veronica but that plan backfired. It definitely proved that everything that was done in the dark would come to the light.

"Come on bro I'll ride with you. Torre will make sure to drive around long enough to calm the misses down and give us a chance to make it in before her." Malachi said.

"Go ahead baby. I'm so sorry for all of this. Had I known I wouldn't have called you tonight." Sarita apologized.

"It's not your fault you were just trying to help make things better. This was all me and I have to own it. I should have just told Veronica but I wanted to fix it." I said worn out over the whole ordeal.

"Why are you apologizing to him mama! I'm the one that just had a baby and got attacked by his wife. He continues to lie to her when I know that he wants me!" Adrian jumped in.

"I can't believe this. Everything you told me when I visited you at the jail was all a lie? You never meant to make amends with your sister did you?" I asked her. It all made sense to me now and I had fallen once again into a trap.

Adrian didn't respond right away and I knew that I needed to leave. I really didn't expect a response and her silence was enough clarification for me.

"Let's go Kai." I said heading towards the door.

My head wasn't focused enough to drive so I threw Malachi my keys and got in on the passenger side. I couldn't make sense of anything except me making things right with my wife. Here I was a prominent pastor and bestselling author and my life was in shambles. How was I going to continue to lead a church and I couldn't even lead my family.

I used to have the mindset that I didn't care what people thought about me but once I got an understanding of who I was and what I was put here to do, my mindset had to change. I was supposed to be leading people to Christ not away from them but the way things had been happening lately I didn't know if I was worthy enough to be leading God's people.

"Man Malachi I have a wife and a baby mama and my baby mama is also my sister-in-law." I said to him hitting my head on the headrest.

"That sounds like one of those urban books T be reading sometimes." He laughed. I wished I could join in with him but I didn't find anything that was funny.

"How did my life get here? Was I that bad of a pastor?" I asked still with my eyes closed.

"Since when does the enemy bother you because you are out of the will of God? It's only when you are in His will that the attack comes. You know that because you taught that to me." He said making plenty of sense.

As long as you were playing for team Satan he rarely bothered you but as soon as you were all in for God here he comes. But then there were times that it wasn't even Satan it was God and we were giving him props for something that he had no authority in.

God doesn't tempt us but He will certainly give us test that we need to pass in order to get to the next level.

"Well the way I feel right now if God is preparing me for a new level I don't want to go." I said honestly.

"That's not how it works and you know it. When you made that confession and covenant with God that was it." I knew he was right but I didn't want to deal with that right now.

    Before I knew it we had made it back to my house. The once warm and welcoming house was now cold and bitter and had Veronica not given me the orders to beat her home I wouldn't be here right now. But the side of her that I witnessed tonight let me know that she wasn't playing. All of the years that we have been together I had never seen her get that mad and lay hands on someone but tonight my wife was in rare form.

Malachi and I sat in the car for a few minutes stuck in our own thoughts before he spoke.

"Do you think that's really your son?" he asked me.

"Did you look at him? He looks just like all of my other kids when they were born. He and Christian could be twins right now. I don't know what to do but man I can't not be a part of his life." I said.

"Yo man are you serious? How do you think Veronica and the kids are going to feel if you walking around here with a baby by their aunt? That makes them not only first cousins but siblings! This is definitely like one of those urban reads." He said shaking his head. I could tell by the look on his face that he was serious but so was I.

"Look I don't believe in being an absent father. It's not like I intended on cheating on Veronica. You know I would ever do that but Kadesh didn't ask to be here and I can't turn my back on him. The reason Sarita called me was to have Veronica and I come down there to talk to Adrian about what we were going to do when she went back to jail." I informed him.

"So why was it that you were there and not Veronica?"

"With everything she has been dealing with I didn't want her to have to deal with this. I didn't think that she could handle it and think rationally. I guess my assumptions were right." I said.

"Nah. I think that had you given her the benefit of the doubt and talked to her you would have given her the option of choosing what to do. You took that away from her when you chose for her and honestly you chose wrong on this one."

I knew that he was right but how many times do we act on impulse during difficult times thinking that we can fix something but we end up making it worse. I thought about what he was saying and this was why I thanked God for a brother like him. He not only stood by me when I was right but he wasn't afraid to tell me when I was wrong. I learned a long time ago that if everyone is agreeing with everything we do then they don't have our best interest at heart. So of us have people in our lives that can see us getting ready to jump in front of a train and tell us to make sure we smile before we jump instead of pulling us back. Those type of friends aren't the ones I needed.

"Thanks for that man. You are absolutely right I dropped the ball on this one."

"Yeah but just make sure you do everything that you can to pick it back up. It may take some time but don't give up. Veronica loves you and I saw that tonight no matter how upset she was with everything."

"You sure? Cause the way she elbowed me said otherwise." I said as I rubbed my side. That was the first time that she had ever put hands on me and I prayed that it never happened again. I felt bad for Adrian because I know she was going to be in pain for at least a week.

We sat outside for a little over an hour and a half. I texted MJ to find out if everything was ok and he assured me that it was. He was just worried about his mother. I let him know that I was outside and that we would talk in the morning. The next day was Saturday so he didn't have to worry about getting much rest for school.

   Almost two hours later headlights flashed behind us as Torre and Veronica pulled in the driveway. I had finally calmed down and here I was getting nervous all over again. It was kind of like when you were a kid and your parents told you that they were going to whip you but didn't do it right away. Hours and sometimes even days went past and just when you thought they had forgotten about the punishment here they come to make good on their promise.

We watched as Veronica got out and though it was dark the motion sensor lights shined brightly over the garage in around the walkway. The look on her face was unreadable and I didn't know if I should get out and greet her or lock all of the doors and stay put.

The latter seemed like the right thing to do but against my better judgement I opened the door and got out.

"Bae can we talk please?" I said stepping in her path.

"If you don't want to receive a dose of what I just dished out to your baby mama I suggest you get out of my way." She said with such a straight face that I had no choice but to move out of her way.

The three of us looked on as she opened the door and closed it lightly.

"Give her some time Marcus. This was that last drop in her cup to cause her to overflow." Torre said.

"Did she say anything to you?" I asked. Any information on how to fix this was greatly appreciated and I needed to know what to do.

"Not one word. I did all of the talking as she just cried."

That broke my heart even more to know that my wife was hurting yet again and I couldn't be there for her. I wish Iesha had just stayed where she was instead of coming back to wreck what we had built. But that's just how demons do though. They may leave but they roam trying to find somewhere else to go and when they can't find it they return to where they left from. And God help us when they do because you better believe that they are going to return with seven more demons worse than them and they each will bring seven with them and so on. You would end up worse off than you were before.

"I don't know what to do yall." I said leaning against the car.

"This is going to require lots of prayer and fasting cause this is all bad. I still believe in God though." Malachi said.

"Oh I almost forgot. How did you know where we were?" I asked. No one said anything at the hospital and I was surprised to see them there. With so much going on I had forgotten to ask.

"MJ called us. He said that Veronica said she had to come up to the hospital to check on one of the members and when she asked him to watch Christian she didn't look like her normal self. He couldn't leave the kids so he called us." Torre said.

"That boy knows his mother better than I do these days." I confessed.

"He's a smart young man and considering both he and Lai made some big mistakes I couldn't ask for a better father for our grandchild. That's going to be your biggest supporter right now because he knows how to be neutral." Malachi said.

"Yea I'm definitely proud. Well it's late let me get in here and see what it is I need to be doing. I know I'm probably going to have to sleep on my couch in my office for the night."

"The night?" Torre laughed. "Try a few days or maybe even week. Shoot the way your luck is set up maybe a few months."

"Really T?" Malachi asked.

"What?" she asked shrugging her shoulders.

"Don't pay her any attention. But look can we borrow one of the cars to get home? We drove together and then ended up driving you and V here." Malachi asked. I had forgotten that part.

"Yeah take my car that's fine."

"Thanks bro. I'll drop it back off tomorrow after we go pick ours up."

"Alright. Thanks again for everything." I said giving Torre a hug and shaking Malachi's hand as we heard a crash and scream.

"You need us to stay?" Torre asked.

"No I got it. As long as I stay out of Mayweather's way hopefully she will calm down." I said walking off as they got into my car and pulled out into the street. I may have sounded confident but on the inside I was nervous that I would be catching rounds two through twelve that Adrian should have gotten.

Jesus take the wheel.

Chapter Four

Adrian

I knew that I was wrong for everything that had transpired but what's done was done and there was no taking it back. Did I feel bad about it? At first I did when I found out that none of the things that happened to me were Veronica's fault but that all flew out of the window when I watched Marcus run out of the jail a few days ago to go be with his wife.

From the moment I found out that he had accepted my invitation to come speak with me in the jail I felt some sense of hope. Not that we would be together but that he would be understanding and feel some kind of sympathy for me. I had poured my heart out to him and as soon as Veronica needed him he was gone. Just like my father.

Maybe it wasn't fair to feel like it was Marcus' fault that Clarence wasn't around. As a matter of fact I knew it wasn't fair but I still felt like once again another man had left me hanging for my sister. Even Keith was starting to feel bad for her and wanted her back home with her family. That's exactly why I constantly played on his emotions.

Whenever I would not call for a few days or I had an attitude with him I made him feel like it was Veronica's fault. If he hated her I felt like he would stay true to me so each time he started to get a conscience I would add fuel to the flame. He was not about to abandon me too.

From the first time I met him I knew that he was easy prey. I just had no idea that he was that easy. One look at my body I knew that I had him and when we slept together that solidified that bond. No matter what plans I came up with he was down for it in hopes that my love would deepen for him. That would never happen but he didn't need to know that.

    I looked down into my arms as my son squirmed around like he wanted to wake up. I guess he knew that it was almost feeding time. Admiring his curly mane, iced coffee complexion, and beautiful eyes caused me to fall in love with him as soon as I saw him. It saddened me to know that I wouldn't be able to be with him after tomorrow because I would be hauled back off to jail until my trial.

I didn't want my mother taking him with her so I made sure to speak with the patient representative as soon as she left after the fight. I asked to her make sure she put in my records that Marcus was to get our son once I was gone. Being the type of person everyone says he is I knew that he would never let his own flesh and blood be raised by someone else.

    I still couldn't believe that I was jumped right after giving birth but Veronica better hope I don't see her again anytime soon. The only reason she got the upper hand was because I was still weak and not feeling like my regular self. I wished I could see her face when they brought the baby right to their front door. They wouldn't dare turn their backs on a baby especially like that.

Once Kadesh's feeding and changing was done and he was fast asleep I put him back in his bassinet and closed my eyes. Soon visions of Marcus and Veronica fighting filled my dreams. That was until they stopped and it was like they were looking at me and laughing right before they turned to each other and shared a kiss so passionately that I felt it even in my spirit.

    I woke up suddenly and knew that this wasn't going to end the way that I wanted it to.

Chapter Five

Veronica

I woke up the next morning praying that the events from last night were all a bad dream but when I looked around the room and saw the empty space in bed beside me and the sweat suit from last night I knew it was real.

Flashbacks from the time Marcus received that phone call all the way up until I got home and smashed our wedding pictures all over the place took me to a place that I didn't want to be in. The smug look on Adrian's face when I walked in was like she was glad that I had caught Marcus there. I figured that was why she left a visitor's list at the nurse's station. She wanted me to be able to know where she was. Like she was counting on me to be there

The question I had was why though. This woman had it out for me so bad and I didn't know why. At first I thought it was because of Iesha but then the way she looked at Marcus tonight I knew it was about him. When I sat and thought about it every time she was around Marcus she gave him the same look. A soon as she started coming to the church she always made it a point to get in his face before leaving. I didn't think anything of it at the time but now I see I missed the warning signs.

She was so subtle with it unlike a few of the other women who flat out tried to get close to him and made no attempt to hide it. Needless to say they don't attend anymore. Then once she started bringing

Keith with her I really had no reason to pay attention. I trusted my husband so I never worried. That was until now.

Marcus being so sneaky about everything was out of the ordinary for him but once I set eyes on that baby I knew why he didn't want me at that hospital. That baby looked just like Christian and our other children and I couldn't deny that he was the father. If nothing had hurt me before, seeing him smiling while holding that child did something inside of me to cause me to snap.

Go knows that it wasn't the baby's fault but there was no way that I was going to willingly accept him. Not the way that he got here. To know that Adrian had had my man and it was something that he wanted like she said broke me.

Forcing myself to get up I went into our bathroom and stripped out of my clothes. Looking into the mirror I let the tears fall. Was this my punishment for everything I had done in my past? Hadn't I turned from my evil and wicked ways and was walking bolding for Christ? This had to be my punishment and I didn't know if I was strong enough now to just deal with it.

Getting into the shower I closed the glass door and just stood there letting the hot water attempt to wash away everything. Every pain I was feeling I wanted it to be gone. I needed it to be gone.

The tears wouldn't stop as I broke down in the tub and cried until I had no more tears left. I got myself up and washed up the best that I could. My energy was low and I all I could do was dry off, put on a long cotton t-shirt and climb in my bed. I made sure that my bedroom door was locked because I didn't want to be bothered. Not with Marcus not with the kids and definitely not with the hatred that was building up inside of me.

******

I was so tired of keeping myself cooped up in this room that it was beginning to make me sick. Answering my phone was a thing of the past. I had all calls forwarded to my assistant to handle and had her cancel any appointments that were on my calendar. It wasn't a secret anymore about the things that were going on in my household and almost everyone respected us enough to give us our privacy. Though there were some who still tried to call or come by just to be nosy. The paparazzi outside of the church and our house had dwindled down but a few still hung around to see what they could catch. We weren't even big time celebrities but this scandal was even better to some than the TV show.

They were definitely not catching me because I had been inside of our home since my release from the hospital. I hadn't even gone to church and I knew I needed to be there. You would think that after being locked away all of that time that I would want to be around others, especially my family, but that wasn't the case. I had gotten so used to talking with God in my alone time at that house and hearing His voice calm me that I thought it would continue when I came home. But He hadn't said a mumbling word to me since.

Of course I knew that He was right there but I needed to hear the voice of God in order to understand what I needed to do next. When I was locked away from the outside world there wasn't a day that went by that I didn't hear His comforting words. Telling me to hold on and to not give up, bringing scriptures back to my remembrance so that I would be encouraged. Making me laugh when He would remind me of certain things that had gone on in my life when I was happy. I knew that He wanted me to remain in that happy space so why had He stopped talking?

    I flipped through the channels not really paying attention to what was on. My mind was focused on the state in which my once happy marriage and family was in. I wasn't naïve to think that we would never go through anything in life but God knows I never imagined this would be how I ended up. The decisions I had made so many years ago had come back to haunt me in such an unimaginable way.

People always say that had they known back then what they knew now they would have made different decisions. Contemplating my choices I honestly couldn't say if I would have changed them or not because even though I feel like I'm living in hell right now, there was such a hold on me back then that I enjoyed it. I know I wasn't the only one who felt that way but I may have been the only one who was honest enough to admit it.

Forget what you heard, sinning was so much fun because I was feeding my flesh on a daily. Thinking that I could "do me" for as long as I wanted to and when and if I decided to turn my life over to God all would be forgiven. All was forgiven, even cast into the sea of forgetfulness, but I still had to pay for those mistakes. And boy was I paying in a way never thought possible. I guess once I made my confession to God and started to live my life differently that wasn't enough to really make the devil mad. It was when I decided to finally confess to myself and let God clean me up that he started feeling some type of way.

Being honest with Marcus was just the icing on the cake and it was game time.

The night I finally told Marcus everything I knew that he would leave me for sure. Finding out the woman that you fell in love with was carrying such a horrible secret like that for all of those years and then having her secret come put us out on front street should have made him walk away and never look back. But the God I serve had sent me such a man after His own heart that he didn't see who it was that I used to be, he just saw me the way God looked at me. Pure love and adoration always reflected on his face when he looked at me but these days it was long gone.

    I knew that somewhere in my husband there was a part of him that blamed me for this happening although he never uttered a word about it. Come to think of it words were far in and between with us. Especially since that child was living with us now. Just the sight of Kadesh makes me sick and I know that it wasn't his fault that he was born into this world. But to know that the man I loved with every fiber of my being had created another child with someone other than me while we were married took me someplace that I didn't like to go.

No he didn't know that this was going to happen or that she was my sister but I didn't understand how he could love a child that he knew caused me so much pain. Letting the thoughts take over I never realized that I had fallen back asleep.

My phone ringing caused me to I wake up out of the slumber that I was in. I had been asleep and locked up in my room for days. I just couldn't find it in me to want to do anything but cry and sleep. No praying, no eating, no interacting with my family. I just wanted to be alone.

Not wanting to open my eyes fully I grabbed it off of the nightstand and placed it to my ear.

"Hello?" I said groggily.

"Hey boo did I wake you?" Torre asked me.

"Yeah but I need to get up anyway. I need to tend to Christian. When I came in the other night I lost it and fell asleep in all of my clothes. I was hoping all of this was all a dream but I was wrong." I said getting up and sitting on the side of my bed.

Before Torre had a chance to respond there was a knock at my bedroom door.

"Let me call you right back T." I said not waiting on her to respond as I hung up. Something in me was telling me that I was a to get hit with something else and just wasn't ready. The old folks said when it rained it poured they couldn't have been any more correct. My life was a straight hurricane and the storm was getting stronger.

Walking over to the door I unlocked and opened it to find a weary looking Marcus standing before me.

"What?" I asked sucking my teeth with much attitude. I didn't even move to allow him to come in the room.

"Bae I need you to come downstairs. We have company and this is something that needs our attention." He said walking off back down the steps before I could decline.

I thought about just getting back in the bed but when I heard the unfamiliar voices I went and washed my face and slid on a pair of shorts. My appearance was the last thing on my mind so I didn't even bother trying to be presentable.

Taking a deep breath I made my way down the steps and followed the voices into our living room. When I rounded the corner I saw Marcus along with our children, a white woman that I had never seen before, and Sarita even had the nerve to be here. I was so livid that I almost missed the car seat that sat on the floor by the unfamiliar woman.

"I know good and well yall didn't bring this baby in my house." God knows I had an arsenal of curse words locked and loaded but I didn't want to go there with my children in the room.

"Ron baby let us explain." Sarita started.

"Sarita what are you even doing here? Shouldn't you be somewhere tending to your precious daughter?" I said calling her by her first name. I wanted so bad to be able to call her my mother but the wounds were too fresh and I had no idea at this point if I even wanted to be involved with her.

"I'm here because I'm trying to make this right baby. Please let me help." She begged while I remained unmoved.

"You have helped enough and it's time for you to go." I said.

"Maybe I can assist here." The lady spoke up.

"And you are?" I questioned with a slight roll of my neck.

"My apologies. I'm Janice Cleveland from the Department of Family and Children's Services." She introduced herself.

I stood there with a blank expression on my face waiting for her to tell me why she was there.

I guess she picked up on what I was waiting for because she continued.

"Well I'm here because I received a call from one of the patient representatives over at the hospital and she explained to me the situation with Adrian having to return back to jail once she was released from the hospital. In her notes Adrian made it clear that Marcus was the biological father of Kadesh Machi Millhouse."

You could have knocked me over with a feather when this woman stopped talking. Adrian had the audacity to not only give her child Marcus' last name but she even took it a step further and gave him the same middle name as our son Christian!

"WHAT?" everyone said in unison. Dynasty stormed out of the room and I wanted to follow suit but I had to find out why this woman was here.

"Look let's cut to the chase. Why are you here? I know it's not to just tell us this child's name." Marcus finally spoke up.

"Well being that Adrian was discharged and taken back to jail we had to place the baby. Now normally in these situations the mother's don't list a father or they have some other family that they want the baby to go with like their mother. Adrian decided that she wanted her son to be with his father."

"Hold on. Hold on! You mean to tell me that Adrian turned over custody to Marcus? I can't believe this girl. I told her that I would take him and not to do this." Sarita spoke up.

"According to these papers full custody was given to Marcus. I have copies for you as well to sign and everything will be final. Now mind you whenever Adrian comes home she can try and get custody of him back." Janice said passing the papers over to Marcus along with a pen.

I watched as he read over everything and then he looked up at me. The look on his face held nothing but sorrow and it was at that moment that I knew things were about to take a change for the worse. Still I grilled him and dared him to sign those papers.

Holding my gaze for a few more seconds he turned to look at the baby that Sarita had taken out of his carrier and was now feeding. My eyes watered as I got another good look at that baby but I refused to let the tears fall. He looked so much like our children it was uncanny. Before I knew it Marcus was signing the papers and handing them back over.

To say that I was in shock would be an understatement. What happened to being one and discussing things and making decisions together? Marcus wasn't making a simple choice like what to cook for dinner. He was choosing to have his illegitimate child live up under our roof. Not just any illegitimate child but one that he had with my sister!

"What happened to us making decisions that involved our family together?" I asked giving him the hand signal to not even try to respond as soon as he opened his mouth to speak.

"Since you making choices alone I'm going to make one alone too. I'm done." I said walking out leaving everyone standing there.

Chapter Six

Present Day.....

Marcus

I didn't know what I was being punished for but God was giving it to me. Just when I thought things would be looking up I get something else thrown at me that sends me back to square one.

First my wife tells me that she was once in a relationship with a woman who tries to come back and rekindle some old flame. Then my sixteen year old son gets his girlfriend pregnant, and if that isn't enough I'm sitting here looking into the face of both of my three month old sons. One by my wife and the other by her sister.

    The day that the woman from DFCS came to the house with Kadesh in tow I knew it was going to be some mess. There was still part of me though that was holding out hope that there was a ram in the bush that everything was going to be ok.

I knew that when I signed those papers there was a chance that I would lose my wife but I couldn't have a child of mine go into the system. We had so many children and adults in our church alone who experienced that and I don't know what I would do if I allowed that to happen to one of my own. None of our other children ever had to endure it and I wasn't about to let Kadesh do it either. None of this was his fault.

When Veronica said she was done I was so scared that she was going to leave the house but so far she hadn't. She carried on as if I was invisible. Slowly but surely she came back around and was doing her motherly duties but as far as being my wife and support she was having none of that. I couldn't get her to say two words to me and every time she looked at Kadesh her eyes would water.

She didn't go outside of the house unless it was for her or Christian's doctor's appointments and even then it wasn't long. Torre had tried coming to visit her but she didn't even want company. Every time I turned around Adrian was calling the house, my cell, and even the church for me and every call would go unanswered. Because I had her blocked she started having different people call on three way. Once I found that out I began blocking those numbers as well. I just wanted my life back and she wasn't allowing that to happen.

"Hey Daddy. What you doing sitting in here all quiet?" Dynasty asked as she came into the family room taking me away from my thoughts. She grabbed Christian from my arms and started playing with him.

I didn't miss the look of disappointment that flashed across her face when she looked at a wide awake Kadesh. He studied her face for a few seconds before giving her a toothless grin that caused her to smile just a little at him.

"I'm just thinking baby girl that's all. Have you and your sister thought about what it is you wanted to do for your upcoming birthday?" Hopefully just by mentioning a party it would brighten her day as well as get my mind off of everything.

Out of everyone, including me, Dynasty had been taking everything the hardest. Destiny had always been the one that was the closest to their mother but ever since Veronica had gotten kidnapped it was Dynasty that it affected the most.

Just like I had figured the topic of a birthday celebration had lightened her mood.

"We thought that since we never did get a chance to go on our family vacation and Cadence will be one in a few months, then we could possibly just wait and celebrate it all together. Hopefully by then you and Mommy will be ok again and Christian will be a little bigger too." She said. It didn't go unnoticed that she didn't mention Kadesh but I chose not to address that right now.

It wasn't a secret how uncomfortable it has been for everyone to deal with an illegitimate child, especially while being in a leadership position in the church, but I didn't want anyone to treat him any differently. Children could tell when they weren't wanted and I never wanted any of my children to feel that way. Besides Kadesh wasn't conceived willingly but never the less he was now here and a part of this family.

"That sounds like a plan. Just let your mother and I know where and what it is that you want to do and we can start planning." I told her as her smile was replaced by another look of sadness.

"What's wrong baby?" I asked.

She paused for a few seconds before she asked me something that even I didn't have the answer to.

"Daddy are you and mommy going to get a divorce?" Dynasty asked with tears beginning to pool in her eyes. Before I had a chance to respond Destiny walked in.

"Hey Daddy! Hey sissy!" she said bouncing into the room. Taking Kadesh out of my arms she kissed him all over his face as he cooed like he had so much he wanted to say to her.

Dynasty didn't even wait for an answer to the question that she had asked as she got up and handed me the baby again and walked out.

"I hate that I don't know how to help my own sister feel better." Destiny sighed.

The way she had fixed her lips into a pout caused the dimple in her cheek to deepen. It was funny how Destiny and Kadesh both had a dimple in their left cheeks and Dynasty and Christian's were located on the right side of their faces.

"All we can do is pray that God heals this situation sooner than later." I said propping a now sleeping Christian on my shoulder.

"So are you?" Destiny asked me.

"Am I what?" I had no idea what she was talking about.

"Getting a divorce."

"So you heard your sister huh?" I wanted to know.

"Yea that's why I came in here. I know that she asked the question but I don't think she is ready to hear the answer just yet."

"And you are?" I asked. For Destiny to be so young she was definitely wiser than her young fourteen years.

"Daddy I trust God. I know that He will see us through this and everything will work out. I just hate seeing everybody walking around here like they are on eggshells.

Mommy is barely talking to you and she is always crying. MJ has his own family that he has to think about as well as school and work. Dynasty always has an attitude whenever anything pertaining to Kadesh, Auntie Adrian, or GiGi is brought up. And because you are the head of our household, you can't really focus on leading us because you are broken and don't know how to even lead yourself." She ended and quickly covered her mouth.

"I'm sorry daddy for that last part." She apologized. I couldn't even get mad at her because everything she had just said to me was the honest to God truth and I couldn't fault her for telling it.

"No apologies needed Des. You are absolutely right. I'm the one responsible for covering and protecting my family and I have really been doing a poor job of that lately. I need to get it together." I said wiping my hand down my face. These burdens were so heavy that I didn't know if I was coming or going some days.

"Well to answer you and your sister's initial question, I don't know what's going to happen. I love your mother with everything in me and I never wanted anything like this to happen. Some days I feel like we can make it and we have a chance and then other days I feel like it's a wrap.

If someone would have told me that the enemy would be able to come in and destroy my house the way he has been doing for almost a year now I would have told them to go get evaluated for a crazy check. Not because I feel we are exempt from trials and tribulations but because of how it's all playing out."

I wouldn't dare tell her that there are times that I blame her mother for this. Veronica wasn't the cause of the state of disarray that our family was in and I knew it deep down in my soul, but old Lucifer knew how to twist a situation and paint a picture of deception so clear that you start believing what he want you to. He uses that saying, 'Seeing is believing' to his advantage a lot and we let him. Once he finds out what it is he can show you to distract you from what God has already spoken to you, he feels like he has the upper hand.

We are very visual creatures. If we don't see something then it must not be true. I believed that was the main reason we have so many people who don't believe or trust God the way we need to, because we can't see Him or His promises. No matter how many times we hear God tell us that He has already worked things out on our behalf we still want to see it. Even bad things we want to see not realizing that our eyes are the ones deceiving us all along.

"Mommy loves you daddy and I know that you can work this out." She said getting up and taking both boys out of the room.

"Where are you going with my boys?" They were my comfort right now as well as my company because I didn't want to be alone.

The more time I spent to myself I know I should have been using it to get in God's face but I didn't have it in me. As long as I had been in ministry I didn't know what to say to God these days. I could have been using this time to pen another bestseller but the words just wouldn't flow. There was a serious disconnect in my life and if I didn't get connected again and fast I was going to lose one of the most important things to me. My wife.

"You need some time alone to talk and work things out." Was her response as I followed her gaze to the door where Veronica stood.

Chapter Seven

Sarita

I know that I didn't make all of the best decisions during my life but some of the ones I did make I thought they were for the benefit of helping others, especially my children.

It was so hard leaving Veronica behind and although I know Mrs. Verna had explained it to everyone else, my daughter had yet to hear the full story. It was best that she heard it from me but every time I attempted to talk to her either I froze up or something got in the way. I knew it was nothing but the devil that was preventing this conversation from happening. As long as Veronica could assume and not know the full truth he could play her like a fiddle.

    The way Marcus and my grandbabies were suffering as well hurt me even more. I knew that soon I needed to help my daughter come into the truth so that she could get her family back on track. And if the information I was about to receive was what I had been praying for then that would be the first step to reconciling this mess.

To say that I was shocked would be an understatement as I left my first meeting and headed towards the jail to see Adrian. I knew it wasn't visiting day but I had a few people that I knew who worked on the inside of the jail and they were able to pull some strings.

The way my anger was set up at this very moment I was not waiting another week and a half to lay into Adrian. I don't know where I went wrong with her but she was no longer that sweet and innocent daughter I had raised. It was like once she found out about Clarence and Veronica she was set on revenge. It wasn't until recently that this information had gotten back to me when I visited Chicago after seeing the drama unfold one Sunday.

    I went to the church where I had first met Mrs. Verna all those years ago and was able to get her address. When I finally got a chance to sit down and hear of all of the things that my daughter had gone through in my absence it broke my heart and I was determined to right my wrongs.

When I was called to meet the social worker at my daughter's house so that Marcus could sign the papers for Kadesh I stuck around after everything was done because I needed some answers. For the life of me I couldn't understand why Adrian had changed her mind about me having the baby. Something just wasn't adding up.

I asked Marcus what happened when he went to see her at the jail before he got the call that Veronica was found and I almost hit the floor when by the time he went over the conversation they had.

He told me Adrian revealed that she was in a relationship with Iesha as well and once she graduated the academy she was on a mission to find her father and sister and get them back. Iesha didn't know who she was at first and she just made it seem like she was out to get Clarence for what he had done to her although she didn't go into detail of what it was he did.

I sat there as he told me that she didn't know that Clarence was going to die that night and by the time they went back for Veronica she had already left Chicago.

Now what confused me about this story was why no one thought to think that Adrian would have been way too young to have been a police officer at the time all of this was supposed to happen. Veronica and Adrian were a little over seven years apart and during that incident Adrian would have only been around thirteen years old. So there was absolutely no way that she could have been there.

I figured that in order to make her story seem plausible she had to do some digging on that case once she did get the information she needed and found Iesha they came up with that story. It was so much going on that no one even thought about thinking of the age difference. I had to give it to them both though, their scheme had almost worked but you have to wake up pretty early in the morning to get this old geezer. Where poor little Keith came in at I don't know but he was just another casualty in the war that Iesha and Adrian waged.

 I was concerned as to where he was because he had been really quiet and no one had found him since he dropped Veronica off at the hospital. The police were still searching for him and as of right now there were no leads. Something was telling me that he would be popping up when we least expect it and we needed to be prepared for his return.

*****

I pulled up to the correctional facility and ended my call with Verna. I had to fill her in on everything that I knew so that she help me out with Veronica. I just prayed that it all worked out in the end and God was able to get the glory out of this whole thing.

It took me awhile before I was allowed to meet with Adrian in a private room but after about an hour or so an officer escorted her in. I watched as she sat down across from me with a smug look on her face like she didn't have a care in the world. The beautiful woman that I once knew was now gone and it was just a mean, nasty, and spiteful individual sitting before me. All in all she was still my child and I loved her.

"How are you?" I asked trying to break the ice. I didn't even know where to begin with her.

"Cut the crap mama and just get to the point." She said startling me but I wasn't about to back down from her. I was the mother and she would still respect me.

"Let me tell you one thing. I am still your mother and you will respect me. So that little bad girl attitude you have been accustomed to or whatever demon you are letting take over better fall back." I said invading her space so she knew that I wasn't playing.

I watched as the color drained from her face and it was then that I knew she didn't want none of me.

"If you lie to me about anything I ask you right now you better believe you will rot in this prison and that precious little baby of yours will never know you exist." I said pulling an envelope from my purse.

"What's that?" she sked me.

"We will get to that later but right now I want to know why you hate your sister so much that you want to tear her family apart. What has she ever done to you?" I just had to know where this hurt stemmed from.

"She was born first and I had to grow up without a father!" she said as her eyes filled with tears.

"And she grew up without a mother and you don't see her out here making other people's lives a living hell. I gave you everything that I could to make sure you were ok and had everything you needed. I was loving never abused you and was always supporting you. I never lied to you to hurt you but I have hidden some things from you but I did that in order to protect you and your feelings. For that I am so sorry baby."

"You never lied to me huh?" She asked confusing me. I had done all that I could for her and if I lied it wasn't to hurt her at all but to protect her. At least that was what I had hoped.

"Not intentionally." I said to her. I didn't know what she was getting at but I could sense that she was getting irate and I needed to ask her about the information in this envelope.

"Look I didn't come to upset you but I need to know where Keith is. There are some things that he needs to know and he also must be held accountable for his actions." I said pulling out the paper.

"How would I know? Do you not see where I am?" she asked rhetorically looking around the small room.

"I'm pretty sure you have your ways Adrian." I said looking at her and I could tell that she knew where he was she just wasn't telling it.

"Why are you so concerned with Keith all of a sudden?"

"Because he needs to know this." I said as I slid the paper I had in my hand over to her. I watched as she read it and her eyes got big. I just knew that I had her but what she said next just about took my life from me.

"Hmph. You can sneak a DNA test on my child but did you get a DNA test and let Bean know I was his? You know since you around here being Magnum PI and all."

Chapter Eight

Veronica

As I stood in the foyer I listened to Marcus and Destiny talk. It saddened me to know that my whole family was feeling the effects of decisions that I made in my young life. That's what we don't think about when we are out there making stupid decisions when we are younger. We don't think that just because we don't pay for our actions right then that we never will. It may not even come back on us but it could affect our children. Had I understood that back then maybe my family wouldn't be going through hell right now.

I had come downstairs after Mrs. Verna called to tell me she was on the way to our house. It was something very important that she had to tell us and she wanted to do it with the both of us.

Standing by the door I watched the father and daughter interact with one another as well as with the babies. I started feeling bad for not being involved with Marcus as much but not enough to where I was going to start talking to him right away.

Just as Destiny walked by me with the babies in tow she kissed my cheek and the doorbell rang. Mrs. Verna must have been down the street when she called because I didn't even have a chance to let Marcus know that they were on the way.

I paused before I opened the door because I was unsure of what was so important that she needed to talk right away. I didn't have to turn around to know that Marcus was standing behind me because I could feel his presence.

Opening the door I wanted to slam it right back as I looked into the eyes of my mother standing beside Mrs. Verna and her husband. Instead of saying anything to any of them I turned around to walk away but ended up bumping right into Marcus' chest. This was the first time that I had been this close to him in months and as much as I wanted to act like I wasn't moved by him on the inside I was screaming. Not only was my spirit yearning to be reconnected to him once again my hormones was were jumpin!

"When are you going to stop running?" he said calmly. I thought about what he had said and he was right. Every time something got tough I would run away from it instead of facing it. And until I learned to stand in the face of my obstacles I would forever be running and failing the test that God had set before me.

Turning back around I invited them in. I still wasn't fond of being in the same space as my mother right now after that stunt she pulled at the hospital but there was nothing that I could do about it now. We all walked into the living room as Marcus asked if anyone wanted anything. While he went to go get the water boiling for the tea that Mrs. Verna wanted I sat there looking at each of the elders that sat before me wondering what was so important.

Marcus came back into the room a few minutes later with her tea and sat down beside me. I was torn between wanting him to move and wanting him to move closer to me and just wrap me in his arms.

"Ok so what's going on?" Marcus started looking into each of their faces.

"Well for starters you all don't have to worry about Iesha anymore. We got her transferred back to a facility in Chicago where she will get round the clock care. Her mind these days is so unbalanced and there is nothing that we as her parents can do anymore but pray. Those demons have our baby so bound that she doesn't even know who we are anymore. She is always flipping out on people and most days has to be sedated.

I feel so bad because I know this is our fault. Had we gotten her the best care early on in life then maybe she wouldn't be going through this." Mr. Bernard said with tears in his eyes. As much as I disliked Iesha I hated that she was so bad off now and there was nothing her family could do to help her.

"That's sad but please don't blame yourselves. You did all you could for her." I said walking over to Mrs. Verna and giving them both a hug.

I peeped the sadness from my mother but still I was unbothered. Maybe my heart had grown cold but I felt like it had good reasons to.

"Veronica listen. There are some things that your mother needs you to know and I want you to be open minded about it all. In order for you to grow past this individually and as a family you are going to have to talk it out. The last thing you want is to harbor all of this bitterness and miss heaven." Mrs. Verna said.

I knew what she was saying was correct but right now I didn't want to hear it although I knew I had to.

She looked over at Sarita as she went into her purse and pulled out some papers. Before handing them over to us she began to go back in time so that we could get a better understanding of our past.

"It was 1973 when I met your father. Me and a few of my girls had been at the

12th Street Beach all day and were now ready to head back home. I'll never forget my friend Nevetta was driving her boyfriend's new car while he was at work.

    Right before we got to the car Clarence approached me and asked me my name. When I say your father was fine! Good Lord." She said with a faraway look in her eyes as she smiled widely. Just watching her and finally being able to sit in the same room with her gave me that feeling that I had longed for for so many years.

"Anyway. We got to talking and I gave him my phone number. From that day forward we were inseparable. He constantly showered me with gifts and I thought that what he was showing me was love. So after a year of us being a couple we moved in together. I knew that your father was a hustler and I never tried to change that because he never made me feel like I was in competition for his affection.

When I found out I was pregnant with you I was so nervous to tell him because the one time that we did talk about kids he shut me down. He said that because of the life he lived he didn't want to bring a child into the world and he was real specific when he said that he didn't want to chance it being a little girl." She said with sadness in both her eyes and voice.

"Did you know that he was a pimp and selling young women?" I asked her. I just had to know for myself if she had gotten into a relationship with a man that she knew didn't value the worth of a woman.

"Not at first baby. Like I said I knew he hustled but I thought that he was just running numbers and selling a little weed here and there. By the time I found out what he was really doing I was almost ready to deliver you. I hid my pregnancy for a couple of months." She said.

"You seem to be good at hiding stuff huh?" I said with much attitude.

"Come on now Veronica don't do that. We all know you are hurt but take a minute to stop thinking about you right now and put someone else's feelings before your own. You used to be really good at that." Marcus said shutting me up. He was right I was being selfish but I wouldn't let him know that right now. I was still as stubborn as a mule when I wanted to be.

"I'm sorry. Proceed." I said sitting back on the sofa. Marcus shifted in his seat and put his arm on the back of the couch directly behind me like he normally did. Just that subtle movement cause me to have to focus harder on this conversation and less on the smell of his Givenchy Pi cologne. God had to have created that scent Himself!

"Like I was saying, I hid your pregnancy because I was scared that he would make me terminate it and I was right. When I finally told him that I was pregnant I knew that I was too far along for an abortion. So when he suggested we go to the abortion clinic I played along. Just like I knew the doctor told him that I was six months pregnant and he didn't advise me to abort. On the inside I was screaming for joy and prayed that he didn't kill me once we got home." She explained.

To hear that the father that showed me so much love and kindness wanted to abort me was a tough pill to swallow but I was so glad that I had a Father up in heaven that took care of me.

I kept quiet as she continued.

"When we got home that night I just knew that it was going to be a big fight between him and me when he asked me if I knew that I was pregnant. That man could tell when I was lying and I knew the consequences could be harsh but I told him the truth anyway and prayed that I was protected.

    The look in his eyes was unreadable and when he stepped closer to me I flinched because I thought he was about to hit me but instead he wrapped his arms around my body and began to cry. He thanked me for giving him a child and he didn't realize that this was what he wanted until the doctor confirmed it. To say I was shocked was an understatement.

We didn't know that you were going to be a girl and we never talked about what we would do if you were one. So when I went into labor and had you, the moment it was announced you were a girl, your father had the biggest smile I had ever seen on his face. He was so happy and he held you constantly not letting you out of my sight.

So a few years pass by and I become pregnant again. This time I decided to tell him right away because he was so good to you that I knew he would be the same with our next child but I was wrong. He beat me so bad that night that I miscarried. Clarence told me that if I got pregnant again he better not ever find out about it or not only would the baby die but so would I." she paused as the tears consumed her.

I don't know what came over me but I got up and walked out of the room. A few minutes later I came back with watery eyes and tissue for the both of us as I sat beside her. This was the first time that I had been this close to her and to see the same features I had staring back at me did something to me. I didn't speak I just waited for her to get herself together so I could finally close this chapter in my life.

After a few minutes of staring at one another she went on.

"I knew that he was serious and I didn't want that fate. I watched how he took good care of you but the look of disgust that he now showed towards me made me feel less than a woman. Not once did I take that out on you though. I loved you so much and nothing would ever change that." I looked down as she reached for my hand and I surprised myself when I allowed her to hold it.

"By now Clarence was a big time pimp and everybody knew it. I was in so deep now that I was afraid for not just me but you as well and I couldn't leave. He told me that if I ever did and I took you that he would find me and kill us both. So I stayed. Sex was a thing of the past between us and I started to feel like I was just there to take care of you which was fine because you were my baby.

It had gotten so bad that he would bring home some of the women who worked for them and even have them in our bed. Until one day I had become one of his workers. That's how I met Bean." She said looking up at me and everyone in the room.

I could see that Mrs. Verna was just as shocked as I was. Nothing could have prepared me for what she was about to say next.

"Bean was so handsome to me. Don't get me wrong Clarence was fine too but that was just on the outside. Bean was a good man through and through. That's why he and your father clashed."

"How was he a good man when he did the same thing as my father? He was a pimp too!" I yelled and stood up. None of this was making sense to me. I always saw Bean on the blocks with the girls. Shoot Iesha was one of them. Something wasn't adding up.

"I'm not sure what you mean baby. Bean hustled but not women." She said looking genuinely confused.

"When I met Bean he was a numbers runner. Listen you had just turned seven years old and we were throwing you a big party. We had a DJ set up and the whole nine. I had one more gift to go and get you and I ran out to the store before all of the guest arrived.

I got what I needed and on my way out of the store I bumped into Bean. He was so smooth and charismatic that I took a few minutes to talk to him. I even let him know of my dealings with Clarence. A short time after your party I met up with him and one thing led to another. I can't say that I had fallen in love with Bean but I did like him. So when I found out I was twelve weeks pregnant I automatically knew that it was his baby. Clarence and I had stopped being intimate long ago."

"Oh my God." Was all that I could get out. To hear all of this was mind blowing and I swear a motion picture could have been made out of my life. Forget Lifetime we needed a big screen!

"It was at that moment that I knew I had to leave. If Clarence would have killed me because I got pregnant with his child again just imagine what he would do if he knew that I was pregnant by someone else. I had to leave but I was torn. God in heaven knows that I didn't want to leave you baby and if I knew that you would have been safe with me I would have taken you too. But I believed that Clarence would find me and kill the both of us.

The day that I met Mrs. Verna we had just gotten into a big fight. He asked me if I was pregnant and I told him no. He knew I was lying and when he stormed out of the house I grabbed all of the money I could find, grabbed you, and left as fast as I could. The whole time we walked I was clueless of where I would go and if it would be safe to take you with me. That's when I came across the church event.

    Something was pulling at me so strong to stop there for a while and that's what I did. I never intended on talking to anyone. I just wanted to blend in for a while in order to think of a plan. I knew that if for any reason if Clarence saw us he wouldn't dare do anything on the church grounds.

That's when I bumped into Mrs. Verna. She was so sweet and didn't seem judgmental at all. I felt comfortable talking to her and ended up tell her everything. Well almost everything. I kept the secret about Bean to myself and that was one of the secrets that I figured I could take to my grave.

Just when I thought I had it all figured out what I was going to do I saw Clarence drive by real slow. I knew he was looking for me and I panicked. I had to act normal though so I didn't draw any attention to myself. I almost lost it when I saw you running to me and calling my name to come and take a picture with you. There were hundreds of people out there but at that moment I felt like it was just the two of us.

    As soon as we took that picture I was gone. I got us out of there so fast that I never got the chance to get it from the photographer." She said sadly. I could tell that this was hard for her to talk about but I could now see all of the love that she had for me come out in her story. Sarita didn't do the things she did out of spite and how could I blame her for what she had to do.

"Here." Marcus said handing me a picture. Sarita and I both looked at it and immediately she began to cry and the memory of this day came flooding right along with all of the other memories I had locked away.

"Where did you get this from Marcus?" I asked. How was it he had all of the tea and my cup had been empty so long? I guess I didn't allow anyone to tell me anything.

"He got it from me." Mrs. Verna said. "When you all had left I realized that you didn't get the picture. Something was telling me that I needed to get it and send it to you but I realized that I didn't have any information for Sarita. I had given her mine but that was all. I prayed over this picture day and night and when Iesha brought you over for the first time I knew that you looked familiar. It wasn't until that day you came looking for Iesha it clicked." Mrs. Verna explained.

Everything was making so much sense now as they were talking to me. Something in me said that I knew her as well but I had no clue how and I didn't care to ask. This thing was getting so deep and it was like everything was coming full circle.

"Why didn't you tell me if you knew who I was?" I wanted to know.

"Honestly baby you were not in a position that you could receive the truth right then and I didn't want anything to discourage you any further. I prayed that when it was time for you to know that it would be done in God's timing because only He could make it right and have it make sense."

I needed a drink. Not a little shot but a BIG cup of something cause this was 'tew murch' as the twins loved to say. Sitting back down on the couch my mother came and got down on her knees in front of me as she wiped my tears.

"Veronica I know that you may hate me but please understand that everything I did was because I loved you and your sister. I thank God that He kept you safe all of those years even though there was pain you had to endure also. I pray that you can forgive me and we can work on our relationship. I can't expect you to want to jump right in with Adrian or me but I am here baby and I won't leave you ever again." She cried as she opened her arms to receive me.

Without a second thought I fell into her arms and felt every weight that I was carrying be lifted. I cried for the seven year old girl who waited for her mother to return from the bus station bathroom. I cried for the teenager who was pushed into a lifestyle by her father that was unfavorable. I cried for the woman who ran into the arms of another woman because of the lack of a mother figure. I cried for my sister who thought that she was unwanted and felt abandoned. And I cried for my marriage. I had caused so much turmoil just from not having all of the answers or even a few answers. I was in the dark and just like so many others when we don't know what's going on we assumed and caused things to be worse.

    I rested in the arms of my mother for what seemed like forever before I simply said, "I forgive you." Unlike the last time I said it in the hospital, this time I meant it from my heart.

Chapter Nine

Keith

I rode by the Pastor's house in a brand new 2016 Phantom. I knew that my coworkers the police were looking for me but I had peeped game long ago. Even before I left with Adrian and helped her kidnap Veronica I disabled the tracking device on my police issued phone. The only reason I didn't completely get rid of it was because that was how Adrian kept in touch with me and whenever my superior called I still had to put on a front. As long as I stayed in the clear and made everything look normal they had no reason to suspect me of anything.

    The day I dropped Veronica off at the hospital I dipped. No one knew about the house I still had in Houston. That's where I was originally from and my father still lived there. He had long stopped pastoring since my mother passed and I had moved away from home.

I made my way to the end of the next street and parked. I never sat on the same block as their house because I didn't want them to notice the same car. It wasn't out of the ordinary that a car as flashy as this one was seen in the neighborhood. It actually fit in because of all of the people that lived in the area had money.

    The street I was sitting on gave me a clear view of the Millhouse home on the back side. I knew which one was their master bedroom because when they got up in the morning the first thing Veronica did was open their blinds and tie up the curtains. I had picked up on their daily routines before the kidnapping. The only thing was their routine hasn't been the same. I honestly didn't expect them to be after everything so I was glad that I had gotten the information I needed previously.

    I reclined my seat a little and sat back as I thought about everything that had transpired. The last thing that I wanted to do was hurt anyone but for the love of Adrian I would bow up the world and before the feelings were mutual. Or so I thought. It was like she was all into me up until we met Marcus in his office that day.

    When Adrian brought the idea to me she said that we were going undercover because Marcus had been into some shady dealings back in St. Louis. That's the reason that he skipped town and moved to Atlanta. He had gotten married and was not a Pastor. Everything she told me about him got my blood to boiling. It made me mad that a man would put on a front by saying he was a pastor just to cover up his dirt. My father had been in ministry for almost forty years and I knew that he lived that life for real. So when the opportunity presented itself I knew that I wanted in to bring him down.

Now it didn't dawn on me at the time that the information didn't come from our Lieutenant about going undercover like it normally would, it came from her. I guess I was so into her that no matter what she told me I was down.

My parents always told me that a woman would be the death of me but I didn't care bout that. Adrian was going to be my wife and I would stop at nothing to have her.

The service that we attended together the first time something told me that what she was saying about Marcus couldn't have been further from the truth. That man had an anointing on his life like no other. I was able to identify it because it was familiar to me. It was the same anointing my father had.

Right when I was about to back out of the plan and let my superior know that I wanted to no longer be on this case Adrian took me back to her place and put something on me no other woman walking the face of the earth could give! From that point on she had my nose wide open and because she gave me everything I was looking for I made sure to return it. So if outing Marcus was what she wanted to do I was down for my boo.

    I never felt like she had feeling for Marcus. That was up until she slept with him in his office. The plan was that we were going to act like we needed counseling for our upcoming wedding. Pastor and First Lady Millhouse came highly recommended.

When we found out that First Lady had gotten in an accident and couldn't be in the session that only seemed to please Adrian more. She felt like a woman could pick up on another woman's motives before a man could so with her out of the way it would be easier for us to get the info we needed.

It didn't look strange for us to be meeting him alone because we were going as a couple. Had she gone alone it would have been a red flag and someone else from the church would have to be in there with them. When Marcus got a phone call and walked out of the room that's when I got up to put the video camera on his book shelf. I heard Adrian shuffling behind me but I was too busy trying to hurry up and see what it was she was doing.

Once he came back in and we were starting our session I excused myself for a moment. Now the next part of my job was to make sure that their assistant Jonah was distracted because Adrian had a sure fire way that she could get the information we needed. So after a few minutes I excused myself and made my way to the front of the church.

    Jonah was a pretty girl and she was single. I could tell that she was flirting with me and I let her. I didn't shut her completely down but neither did I flirt back because I was here for "pre-marital counseling". The last thing I needed was for her to catch an attitude because I played her to the left from the jump. We carried on a conversation and before I knew it I had been gone for about thirty minutes.

    I thanked her for the water I had initially requested and said my goodbyes. I knew that I had been away longer than Adrian and I had planned so I was expecting her to lay into me once we left. What I didn't expect was to find the woman that I was after on top of another man. To say that I was livid was an understatement. All I could feel was my blood boiling.

Standing there watching how her face twisted up as she enjoyed what it was she was doing took me to another place. I couldn't see his face because the back of the chair was facing the door but I could hear his moaning.

I called her name and she got dressed as fast as she could. I grabbed the video camera and wiped down everything I had touched. From the look on Adrian's face I knew that she had enjoyed being with him and that infuriated me even more. I didn't tell her how I felt but right then I vowed that no matter what I was going to get Marcus one way or the other. He had everything that he wanted and even what I wanted. From that night on things between Adrian and I were strained and I knew it was because of him. The only reason that I continued to help her was because I felt like if I did that would bring us so much closer and we could finally be together the way that I wanted.

    I had just found out that Adrian was locked up by getting into the database. I saw a news report but I had to confirm it through records. I couldn't chance asking one of the other officers so I used my IT skills to override my login before anyone could notice.

Adrian wouldn't be sitting in jail long if I had anything to do with it and right after I dealt with Marcus I was getting my woman out. She was the type that needed to be shown how much someone loved her and I knew by getting her out and handling her business for her would prove beyond a shadow of a doubt that I was the one.

There was a feeling that came over me as I sat there looking at the house. I don't know if it was a warning sign or not but I felt like if I didn't hurry up and get this done I may miss my opportunity to do so. There was a car in the driveway that I knew wasn't theirs when I did my first drive by so I started my car and circled around one more time to see if it was gone. Since it wasn't I decided to go and get me something to eat then I would come back another time. Sooner or later I would get to him but I would just continue to wait patiently.

Had I put my police skills to use I would have paid attention to my surrounding and I would have noticed that the neighbors going into the house beside the Millhouses was none other than Detective Ramos.

Chapter Ten

Sarita

Only God knew exactly how I felt to have my child back in my arms once again. Even though she was a grown woman she was still my child. We cried for what seemed like forever and I knew that there was one last thing that we needed to discuss and that was the information that I held in my purse.

I wiped my face and smiled at my beautiful girl and immediately missed Adrian. I knew that things would never be the way that I wanted them but I was finally able to have a relationship with Veronica and my grandbabies. I had missed her whole life and years from Adrian's but I refused to miss anymore. I just prayed that God would one day repair our whole family and we would be together again. If not I was still at peace.

We had dinner and I noticed that although we were all talking, Veronica and

Marcus would only say a few words to each other and not one time did she look at him. I knew that she was still feeling some kind of way about Kadesh because every time we talked about the kids she would flinch when his name was brought up. Her face told that she didn't hate the baby but she didn't know if she could honestly love him knowing that he was a baby her husband made.

It was time that we talked about the other elephant in the room so I excused myself from the table and went to get my purse. I came back into the room as Marcus was starting to clear the table.

"Um there is something else that we need to discuss." I said nervously fidgeting with the envelope.

"We can go in the living room if this is private." Verna said. I hadn't told anyone about the DNA test that I had done when Kadesh was born.

"No, no that's fine. You both can stay. I consider you family now and I want you to be here." I said as I smiled at them.

"What's going on Ma?" Marcus said to me. It warmed my heart to know that he accepted me even with all of my flaws and past mistakes.

"Well it's about Kadesh." I said nervously looking at Veronica. The look she held told me she was fighting back the urge to walk out so I had to make it quick.

I opened the letter as I explained what it was.

"I may get in trouble behind this if it ever gets out but I took a chance anyway. I don't know the full extent of the relationship between Adrian and that man Keith but if I know my child like I think I do there is more that she wasn't telling us.

The day that Veronica was found and was in labor was the same day that Marcus went to go visit her in the jail."

"Oh did he now?" Veronica said shaking her head.

"It's not what you think baby." He tried to assure her but she wasn't here for it.

"Continue so that I can go tend to *my* baby please." Veronica said rolling her eyes while hitting Marcus with a low blow.

"Don't do that Veronica just hear me out. Anyway I learned from one of the guards that the moment that the detective burst in the room to tell you that Veronica had been found Adrian tried to make you stay by standing up and saying that her water had broken.

Baby girl Marcus had no idea that Adrian was pregnant until that moment and even then his main focus was getting to you. Once he left she made a comment about if Keith was there he wouldn't leave her or their baby." I revealed.

I watched as everyone in the room seemed to be holding their breaths waiting on me to finish.

"Well low and behold two days later she really did go into labor. When I received the phone call I went right to her. I got to the hospital and was stopped by a woman who looked so familiar to me but I couldn't place who she was. Her name was Sandra and she told me that her mother was none other than my friend Nevetta! She recognized me from the many pictures that her mom had of us when we were younger. I had left before Vetta had any children and I never saw her when I returned to Chicago years later.

Sandra told me she worked there in the lab and that's when I knew that God had placed her there specifically for that time. God was always up to something I tell you. As soon as she told me that I knew what I had to do.

I pulled her to the side and told her what I needed done. She said that because her mother spoke so highly of me and missed me so much she would do anything to help. When I called Marcus to come down to the hospital I wanted the both of you to come so I could tell you my plan instead he came alone."

"Why didn't you tell me where you were going Marcus?" Veronica interrupted.

"I didn't want any more stress on you baby. Christian was only three days old and you were finally home resting. I promise you it was no other reason." He assured her as he sat in the seat beside her. To see the love that they both obviously held for one another I knew that I needed to tell them the rest.

"Marcus got there while the nurses were helping her to shower and get cleaned up. I gave him something to drink and handed him to the baby once he was done drinking. I only handed him the bay so that I could slip the can in my purse. Veronica he didn't even want to hold the baby and when he did he was honest and told me he didn't feel a connection. The moment you came in I knew that it was about to be a problem. That was when all hell broke loose.

To make a long story short cause I have been talking so much. I took the can to Sandra after you left and today I got the results of the test I had run." I said handing the paper to Marcus and Veronica.

"What kind of test?" He asked confused. I didn't answer him as I watched the tears fall from Veronica's eyes and she ran from the room.

"Kadesh isn't my son! He's not mine!" Marcus shouted. He hadn't even realized that Veronica had disappeared he was just happy that he didn't have this hanging over his head for the rest of their lives.

"I think it's best that we leave them to work things out. So much has happened and they just need to process things right now." Bernard said to me and I agreed. I knew this was huge and I prayed that it showed Veronica how much I loved her.

The three of us got our things and headed out. We made sure to pray and ask God that now that everything was out that the healing process would now be able to begin and our family would come back stronger than ever.

It wasn't good to rush God but this was one time that I prayed He moved expeditiously.

Chapter Eleven

Veronica

After finally hearing the full story from my mother I had such a better understanding about what went on and why everything happened like it did. We still didn't know exactly how Adrian found out that Bean was her father but we figured she just used her police resources. My mother didn't even know what made her look into it.

Sarita said that when confronted with the truth at the jail Adrian shut down and asked to be taken back to her cell leaving my mother to think about what she had done. Leaving the jail she admitted that she thought about leaving again but just like me she was tired of running from her problems. Even if we didn't work on our relationship she wanted to at least tell me what had happened so that I could now have a chance to decide what I wanted to do going forward. I was never given that opportunity before and she figured she owed me that much.

It was Iesha's father who told us what he thought may have happened. He said that he knew Bean and he was really a good dude. Mr. Bernard wasn't into the streets like that but he had family and friends that were. He told us that once my mother left and he found out that she was pregnant he knew that it had something to do with Clarence. He thought that maybe my father had hurt her in some kind of way so since he took something that he loved Bean was going to take something my father loved.

Iesha said that Bean was mad that Clarence was taking over his streets and taking his girls with him but that wasn't the truth. It was all about my mother and that's all that he wanted. Bean had recruited some of the other girls who were jealous and that's when they killed my father.

It was so much information that was being dished out that I had gotten a headache by the time they were done.

Although I had gotten that part of my life figured out, I still had to figure out what we were going to do about the baby and that's when it really hit the fan!

Marcus decided that everyone should stay for dinner so he ordered in. Neither of us had time to cook anything because it was getting late. After we all ate dinner and talked a little more we sent the kids back upstairs and the last bomb was dropped.

My mother told us that she snuck and had gotten a DNA test done on Kadesh!

When I saw that paper that said Marcus was excluded from paternity and there was no chance that he was the father I thought I would be ecstatic. Instead I felt horrible and ashamed. I had been so mean to a child all because of the circumstances that were thrown at me and it wasn't his fault. Now here I was looking like an inconsiderate fool instead of the loving wife I should have been.

    I ran up to our room and cried for what seemed like forever. I didn't come down even after I heard everyone leave. I was too embarrassed to face anyone. The only person that I knew wouldn't look at me funny or judge me was Torre so I called her.

"Hey my boo! Are you ok?" Torre answered the phone. Her voice went from sounding happy and excited to worried and concerned when she heard me sniffing.

"I've made such a fool of myself! Had I just listened to when everyone was trying to talk to me instead of formulating my own scenarios this wouldn't be happening right now." I cried.

"Sis what are you talking about? What happened? Girl who do I need to fight?" she yelled and it sounded like she was fumbling around.

"Ouch! Shoot that hurt. Where is my shoe?" I heard her say ignoring me on the other line.

"Bae what are you doing? Where you going looking like that?" Malachi said in the background.

"It's about to go down! The keep on messing with my girl and I'm tired of it. I bet it's that ole' no edges having sister of hers. I can't wait to snatch her one good time. She think Veronica got a hold to her but just you wait til this New Orleans Ninth Ward chick get to her!"

"Wait! Torre calm down! I don't need you coming over here I'm fine." I yelled to get her attention.

"Well what in the world you doing all that crying fuh?" she said letting her accent come through. Torre had been away from her home for years but whenever she got excited or upset you could hear that accent strong and mighty.

"I messed up T. I have been so mean to Marcus all this time and to Kadesh and he's not even his father!" I began to cry again. Bright and early Monday morning I was making a call to my OB/GYN cause I needed something to get my hormones under control.

"You lyiiiiiing!" Torre said getting all excited. She made me sick sometimes.

"My mother had a DNA test done and she just showed us the results." I ran down everything to her that my mother revealed to us and by the time I was done this nut was speaking in tongues and praising God. I loved my friend but she could be so extra sometimes.

"So have you had the chance to talk to Marcus yet?" she asked me.

"Did I not just say that once I saw the results I felt so bad I ran out? I called you right away."

"Oh no hunty you better go talk to that man. It's time for you to be a woman and tell your husband that you are sorry and you were wrong."

She was right and I knew it but I couldn't do it tonight. I needed to be alone and finally spend some time with God. It was long overdue. Torre understood and told me that we should go out tomorrow. I needed to get out of the house anyway and I agreed to pick her up. We ended our call and for the first time in months I got down on my knees and prayed.

*****

God knows I didn't want to lose my husband that's why I had to show Marcus instead of telling him. It had been so long since we had been able to spend some alone time together and I was really starting to miss my man. Well he was willing but I wasn't. Not only was my body not the same but neither was my mind after everything happened. I had to get myself together before it was too late.

After last night I felt like I could finally get back to who I was and work to repair my marriage. When I was done praying last night I felt so free and for the first time in a while I felt the presence of God and I knew that everything would be alright soon. I had expected Marcus to come upstairs once everyone had left but he didn't. It was around three thirty when I went downstairs and I heard him praying and crying out to God. It broke my heart and I knew that this was something I needed to make right.

I walked up to Torre and Malachi's house and rang the doorbell. Today was going to be a day of pampering for the both of us so that we could really catch up. I wanted to let her know how thankful I was for her and Malachi for stepping in and helping our family out emotionally and spiritually during these hard times.

People didn't realize how draining things like this could be if it wasn't happing to them and nine times out of ten people were so selfish that they didn't want to be bothered. The Abrams were a different kind of loyal. Not just the type to be there when it benefitted them but when they had nothing to personally gain from it. They did it from their hearts and even after their daughter got pregnant by our son they never changed. It actually brought us closer and we were truly a family in every sense of the word.

"Heyyyyy best frannnnnn!" Torre said opening the door with a bright smile and her arms extended.

"Heyyyy boo!" I said as we embraced and rocked back and forth. We both had tears in our eyes when we parted. It felt so good to be back with not only my assistant but my sister.

"Come on girl before they try to come and find me." She said as we broke out running like teenagers trying not to get caught by our parents. As if we weren't the parents ourselves.

By the time we had made it inside my car we both had to pause and breathe before we could even put on our seatbelts. Between the running and uncontrollable laughter we were about to pass out.

"Girl my behind is too old to be running and laughing at the same time. I gotta pick a struggle Jesus." Torre said making me laugh even harder.

"Please stop I'm bout to be no good fooling with you." I told her finally getting myself together and pulling out of her driveway.

We headed to the mall to get our nails and feet done before making a few stops in Torrid and Victoria's Secret to get me a few smell goods. Marcus loved the way my skin smelled in the Victoria fragrance and I hadn't bought any in a while. I knew that with this scent and the night I had planned, it would have to get us reconnected on more than one level.

After we got a bite to eat at Red Robin we headed back in the direction of our homes, well at least that's where I thought we were going. Torre was driving and she had a sneaky grin on her face.

"Unt uh. What's that look for and where are we going?" I asked looking over at her.

Without a word she turned into a shopping center and parked directly in front of an adult store.

"Oh no ma'am! We are NOT going in here!" I said clutching my imaginary pearls.

"And why not?" She asked while rolling her eyes then answered before I could.

"Let me guess. It's because you are a first lady and first ladies don't do things like this."

"Exactly!" I said huffing and looking at the front of the store. Lord have mercy on my soul because this was bound to be a sin if I stepped in this here store.

"Girl bye! Tell me what's wrong with a wife doing different things to keep her bedroom spicy with her husband? It's not like you and Marcus are shacking or single and fornicating. This is your husband and there is nothing wrong with keeping it interesting with your man.

After all that had been going on you should be trying to beat me to the door. You need to be pulling out all the stops on this one boo for real. Shoot if Malachi finds out I'm here without him he's gonna be mad because I left him at home." Torre said tooting her lips out and I laughed.

"Wait what? Malachi comes with you?" I said shocked.

"Chile yea. It's been times I get home and see that cute little red and black bag on our bed with a white bow and I already know what time it is." She said bouncing in her seat.

"Oh my God Torre!" I screamed as I fell out laughing.

"I bet if you get these goodies for Marcus and have a real nice playlist going he will forget all about that funky little attitude you been having."

    I sat there for a minute as I watched Torre get out of the car and walk inside not caring if I was behind her or not. Looking around to make sure I didn't see any of our messy church members I got out and moved quickly to the door. Walking in I almost turned around and ran home. Forget the car and Torre I was about to be out!

    I looked to my left and saw all of the videos and knew that was not the section I needed to be in. If I could be honest and transparent, part of me felt like a kid in a candy store with all of the possibilities that I could present to my husband. Then there was the part of me that knew my Father was watching me and I wondered if He was shaking his head or cheering me on.

"Sis! Look at this!" Torre said appearing out of nowhere holding up some kind of oil.

"God forgive me and my sister cause we have no business in here." I laughed at her.

By the time we left I had a few things that I did think Marcus would enjoy and I was all about making tonight about him. The younger kids were going to be with Torre and Malachi while MJ and Lailani went their football game at school. I was excited to reconnect with my man again and I just prayed that I wasn't too late.

*****

When I got home Marcus was just getting the kids ready to head out and drop them off. I looked at him and saw the weariness in his eyes and my heart broke. The man that I promised God that I would take care of needed me and I was unavailable. I let my own selfishness and hurt take precedence over what I should have been doing as a wife. I was supposed to have been thankful that I was able to make it back home to my family alive and well along with our son and here I was continuing to be a victim and taking it out on my family. So many times Marcus made things right but now it was my turn to do the fixing.

"Hey." I said as he put the babies in the car.

"What's up?" He said closing the door to his truck. I watched as Destiny and Dynasty looked at us with hope filled eyes and I felt even worse. My actions not only affected my husband but our children and everyone that was attached to us. I couldn't continue to live like this and I didn't want them to either. I was fixing this with God's help and it started with me.

"Um how long will you be gone?" I asked praying that he would be gone long enough for me to set up and not too long to where I would chicken out.

"About an hour. I'm just dropping the kids off and then running by the church to let Deacon Johnson in. After that I'll be back. Do you need anything?" he said opening the driver's side door before getting in but still not making full eye contact with me.

"No just hurry back. Please?" I was desperate now because I was feeling him slipping away from me.

The look of surprise registered on his face before he could hide it and instead of responding with words he just nodded his head. I waved to the girls and prayed that this would bring us back to where we needed to be. The smiles on their faces showed that they were hopeful as they made their way out of our neighborhood.

"Lord please help me fix this." I quickly said before going into the house and setting up.

Chapter Twelve

Marcus

I dropped the kids off at the Abrams' house and headed towards the church. Each time I made this twenty minute drive I felt empty. Empty because I didn't have my right hand girl back like I was used to. When I was weak she was strong and vice versa but it seemed like these days we were both weak at the same time. Crying out to God was hard for me and I didn't know what to do anymore. I was on the brink of losing my marriage at the hands of the enemy and fighting was no longer an option.

When Sarita put everything out there on the table last night I just knew that Veronica and I would be able to jump right back into things but once again I was wrong. I was even more lost than I was before the conversation happened. I happy to finally know that I wasn't Kadesh's father but then I thought about what he would go through without someone who loved him in his life. So many boys grew up without a strong male figure in their lives and I couldn't let that happen to this child. It wasn't his fault that he was brought into this situation. I knew that Adrian would probably not get out anytime soon and if and when they found Keith he would be going to jail too. I didn't know what to so all I could do was pray God came through in the clutch one more time.

    Pulling up to the building where I experienced many moves of God I felt empty and full at the same time if that's even possible. Full from all of the hell that was invading my life and the life of my family. If one more bad thing was to happen I would overflow. Then I felt empty because I missed my wife. Her touch, her smile, her kind words. All of that seemed like a thing of the past and I prayed that after last night we could get that back. I needed her like I needed my next breath and without her I honestly didn't know if I could survive.

Deacon Johnson got out of his car once he noticed me parking in my spot and walked towards me.

"Hey there Man of God. How you doing sir?" he asked me.

"I'm here Deac. Trying to hold on and make sense of it all." I replied honestly.

"As long as you are holding on and not letting go that's all that matters. Just don't let go."

"That's hard somedays when I feel like what I'm holding on to wants me to let go." Rubbing my hand down my face I sighed.

Not responding right away the look on his face let me know he understood what I was saying.

"That's tough Pastor. Especially when it's someone we love more than anything. But does God let go of us when we treat Him like we don't want to be held?"

I thought about what he asked me and it made so much sense. Plenty times we show God that we don't need Him or think that we don't and we try to push away but He loves us so much and knows what's best for us that He can't let us go. And if we are honest with ourselves we really don't want Him to let us go. It just made me think about Veronica even more. She had gone through so much in a short period of time that the way she was trying to deal with it was causing her to push me away but she didn't really want me to give up and in return I was doing the same to her. We were playing tit for tat. If she wasn't strong enough to help us fix this then I had to stand up and be the man that I had always been and get us back on track.

"Deac that just blessed me. Thanks man I needed that."

"No problem Pastor. Sometimes God has to bring things that we already know back to our remembrance. Just know that He is still in control and you have the victory over your enemy. First Lady is still that strong and powerful helpmeet she has always been. She just needs a little help getting back to that place."

"Let me get out of here and head home. I have to get my wife back." I said taking the church key off of my keychain and giving it to him to lock up. I wasn't leaving my house until my wife and I were back where we needed to be. If we had to shut ourselves in then that's what we would do.

"One more thing before you go Pastor." He stopped me.

"Sure what's going on?" I asked. I was ready to leave and go home but I didn't want to be rude.

Deacon Johnson and his wife Mother Johnson had been two of our oldest members and when everything went down in the beginning they were two of the few people who had continue to stand by us.

"This isn't something that my wife or I brought to anyone else in the church. We were having a private conversation at home. I know how you were ambushed the last time and we didn't want that happening again. Mother and I think that maybe you should take a ministry sabbatical. You know not just leave the church but let some of us take over the duties for you and First Lady for a while. Maybe get Minister Malachi and his wife to lead and we can assist them in whatever they need.

    We love you guys and we want nothing but the best for you all. You don't have to decide right now but talk with First Lady and the two of you pray about it ok?" He said making a lot of sense.

    "I hadn't even thought about that but this may be just what we need. I will talk with her and get back to you. Thank you so much Deacon Jones for always having our backs." I told him before giving him a fatherly hug.

"That's what we are here for son. We are family and we are gonna come out of this stronger. Go ahead and get back on home. I'll lock up when I'm done." Deacon Johnson said walking into the church.

I got in the car and thought about everything that he had told me and it didn't sound like such a bad idea.

******

Pulling back up to our home I sat in the car for a few minutes. For the first time in months I was excited to be here again. Each time I drove up it felt like I was driving into a war zone and once the war had calmed down it was just a dead zone but right now it felt like everything had been restored.

I looked at the home that God had blessed us with and thought about how He was with us at every crooked turn or narrow road and I knew that He would still be with us. First I would get Veronica and I back on track and then we would focus on working on the relationship with her sister and maybe even Iesha. I felt like she and her mother were going to be alright now that everything was out in the open but only time would really tell.

Satan thought he had won this battle but he was about to find out that once again he was sadly mistaken. I serve a mighty God and this was already conquered by Him for us!

    I unlocked the front door and smelled that scent that always took me someplace else. It was that Victoria perfume from Victoria Secret. Closing the door and locking it I pressed my back against it and closed my eyes savoring the fragrance and how it made me feel. It had been so long since I felt this close to Veronica and she wasn't even in the room. Or so I thought.

Her presence in the room was immediately felt and when I opened my eyes the breath I was inhaling caught in my throat. The sight before me was like nothing I had ever seen before. Veronica stood at the top of the staircase looking like the angel that she was. Her hair was long and in flowing curls, they reminded me of the way the ocean waves moved in a slight breeze. She had on what looked like a white silk nightgown that hugged her essence as a woman. Nothing or no one could look as beautiful as she did right now. I swear as she moved down the steps it looked like she was blowing in the wind. I had to close my eyes and open them again because I was tripping.

When she got in front of me she uttered not a word as she took my hand and led me to our dining room. Picking up the remote control to the surround sound she hit the power button and Avant crooned through the speakers. Leading me to the table she sat me down in front of a fruit spread of my favorite fruits. The aroma from the sweet mango, kiwi, and strawberries reminded my stomach that I hadn't eaten all day.

"I'm sorry my king." Veronica started and I stopped her.

"No baby. It's-" I started just to be cut off by her in return.

"Let me finish please." She said pleading with her eyes and I had to oblige. I knew that she needed to get this off of her chest in order to begin her healing process and I couldn't stand in the way of that.

"Go ahead baby." I smiled as I wiped the single tear that fell from her eyes.

"I have been being unfair and not really thinking about what you and the kids have been going through too. It's not your fault for all that has happened and it's not right to make you feel like it. I honestly was just thinking about me and what I had went through and it was easier to place the blame on everyone else. I didn't know how to process it and I even blamed God too when I shouldn't have." Veronica poured out to me as she cried.

"Baby I will always be here for you if you just let me. I know it's not easy to deal with everything you had to endure alone but just like God I will never leave you nor forsake you."

"That was so corny." She laughed and so did I.

"I know but it's true." I said getting serious again. "I made a promise to love you and be there for you always. I'm sorry that I missed the mark this time."

"You didn't miss it baby." She paused looking up into my eyes.

"What's wrong?" I knew the look on her face and it told me she was holding something from me. Not like it was something horrible that she was hiding but like she was being mischievous.

Veronica got up as Keke Wyatt took over serenading us and walked over to the other end of the table removing a black and red bag that she had hiding in the chair. My jaws started hurting as I recognized where the bag had come from. I had a feeling that it wasn't Veronica's idea to go to Intimate Pleasures in the shopping center closest to Malachi and Torre's house. He had filled me in during one of our men's fellowships where I was trying to think of different ways to keep it spicy in our undefiled bed.

I watched as she let the melody and the words take over as she moved to the beat while making her way back over to me.

I'm gonna make it rain tonite

I'm gonna make it rain tonite

Im gone make it rain tonite

I'm gonna make it rain tonite

Boy this is what you want

Imma make it storm tonite

Precipitation fill the room

You feel the thunder rollin boo

Feel the rumble when our love collides

Skin to skin gone make you come alive

I watched as my wife began to return from

the place that she had been hiding in for

months and I couldn't wait to meet her again. She closed her eyes and sang the words as if she was doing a duet. Once again I could feel our connection getting stronger and it caused me to stand up and meet her halfway. I may have been rushing but I was still a man so by the time she opened her eyes I stood before her in all of my glory.

Busting out laughing she put her hands on her chest as tears fell from her eyes. Now I don't know about her but I didn't see anything funny it was time to become one for real!

"Baby wait! How did you come out of your clothes so fast?" she asked still laughing and I had to join in.

"Come here." I said to her as she walked into my arms. I felt her heartbeat match mine like it did on our wedding night.

Now God Himself would have to come off the throne and tell me that when I kissed my wife those were not fireworks that I was seeing and hearing and if He did that may be the only time I disagreed with Him. Nothing could make this moment feel any better than it did right now. I didn't know about her but I was ready to see what was in that goodie bag of hers. So picking her up, I carried her upstairs in my arms and prepared to touch a new level of her that had yet to be discovered.

Chapter Thirteen

Keith

When I woke up this morning there was a feeling that I couldn't shake. The only time I felt like this was when I was about to go on a bust. It was like something was telling me not to go do what I was about to but I put the feeling in the back of my mind.

I got myself dressed and grabbed something quick for breakfast before heading over to complete this one last task. Marcus had no idea but this was about to be his last day walking the face of the earth. It was because of him that I had lost everything and he was once again on top of the world.

Deciding to drive back over to their house in the middle of the night just to make sure the car I had seen the other day was no longer there I happened to just sit a while. They had forgotten to close their curtains and blinds all the way last night so when I saw that all was well with them by the performance they were putting on I couldn't take it much longer.

Marcus had managed to have everything that he wanted including the woman I wanted to marry and the child that I wanted to be mine. Since he had taken everything that I had in this world I was about to do the same. I called it a night and headed back to my hideout to wait until morning.

When I got about three exits from their house my phone rang and it was my father. It had been a couple of days since I talked to him and he had been blowing me up ever since. I didn't want to risk him calling while I was taking care of business so I answered.

"Hey Pops what's going on?"

"That's what I need you to tell me." He said in an unusual stern voice. The only time I heard that was when he was upset and I hadn't done anything wrong. At least nothing that he knew about.

"What you mean?"

"Why did your mother and I get a visit from two detectives the other day asking us if we knew about your whereabouts?" He asked,

Had I not already been off of the interstate and stopped at a red light I probably would have crashed.

Trying my best to play it off I asked, "What are you talking about? What did they want?" My nerves were on edge so when the light turned green I pulled over into the Race Track gas station and parked.

I didn't know if I had been found out or not but I had to make sure.

"They came in here asking about the last time we talked to you and if we knew where you were. They said they were looking for you for questioning but they didn't go into details." I felt a little better with that information because it didn't sound like they had any concrete evidence and they were just speculating.

"I have no idea what's going on." I lied.

"Well let me ask you this. Shouldn't they be able to find you if they track your cell phone. I know for a fact that police issued cell phones has tracking on them. And if not then they should know where you were if you were going to work." He was putting too much together and I didn't know how much longer I could stay on the phone with him.

I didn't want to risk getting caught or my opportunity to do what I had to do. I didn't even know if this was some kind of trap and he had the police listening on the phone. If he did then that mean that soon I would be tracked so I needed to end the call immediately.

"Pops let me call you back. I'm about to walk into the station." I said before hanging up on him and turning my cell off. No more interruptions.

I turned on their street and noticed the garage door was open. I never understood why people did that not knowing if anyone would be lurking and waiting behind something just to rob them.

It just wasn't safe but it worked to my advantage.

All of the cars were in the garage as I watched two twin girls rush out trying to make the school bus that had just pulled up. I knew they had a son and I figured either he hadn't left yet or he was already gone. I pulled up a little further so that my car couldn't be seen and got out.

Staying close to the house as to not be detected I slipped right in and positioned myself behind one of the cars and waited.

About fifteen or twenty minutes later I heard the door that led to the garage open and heard the car door open. I peeped my head around the bumper and could see without getting noticed.

"I love you too." Their oldest son said before closing the door and getting in the car that was on the other side of the room.

I was so glad that I had chosen the right car to hide behind. I waited until he had pulled out and the garage door had closed completely before I got up from my hiding place and walked over to the other door. Praying that he didn't lock the door I turned the knob and was thankful that he didn't lock it. I didn't hear the beeping that indicated the code for the alarm needed to be entered in order for it not to go off so I knew that he had forgotten to secure that as well.

As soon as I crossed that threshold and closed the door behind me that wave of uncertainty along with a bout of nausea came washing over me. Once again I shook it off.

Making sure the downstairs was secure I made my way up the flight of stairs. This house was huge! It was decked out and decorated like nothing I had ever seen before. This could have been us but Adrian was playing.

I heard laughing coming from the end of the hall along with a baby crying. From my surveillance I knew that was the master bedroom. Just to be on the safe side I checked all of the other rooms upstairs when I stumbled upon the nursery. I noticed movement in one of the cribs I walked over to it and saw a little boy that looked just like Adrian. He was so chunky and had a hair full of hair. When he noticed me looking over him he frowned. It was like he knew what I was here to do but I dint care.

    I wanted to run out of here with him but he wasn't mine. Adrian made sure to keep rubbing that into my face every chance she got but I wanted her so bad I was willing to do anything to keep her and the baby happy. Maybe once I was done here I would snatch him up and take him with me.

I backed out of the room and made my way to the last room. The door was slightly ajar and I could see Marcus and Veronica talking to each other as she was breast feeding the baby. Not waiting anymore I burst in the door startling the both of them before they had known what was going on. I was about to prove to Adrian that I was holding her down no matter what.

"Looks like all is well again huh?" I said as I pulled my gun out pointing it at the two of them. Baby included.

Chapter Fourteen

Marcus

"Looks like all is well again huh?" I heard looking up from Christian feeding to see Keith standing in front of us holding a gun.

"Oh my God!" Veronica yelled.

"So you're not happy to see me Ron? I thought that by now you would be missing us hanging out." He said with a deranged look in his eyes.

I noticed Veronica look over at her cell phone that was beside her on the nightstand. Not only did I know what she was thinking but so did he.

"Don't you even think about it." He said calling her out.

There was no way that I was about to let him hurt my family so if I had to take a bullet for them I would. I didn't mind dying so that my family could live.

"Where do you think you're going?" he said taking the safety off of the gun.

I knew that there was a possibility that Keith would be showing up soon because we had received a call from Detective Ramos saying they had a lead on him. He said that the other day they thought they had seen him driving past the house real slow as the detective was going into the house next door where they did their stakeout.

After a lot of digging they ended up finding his parents and had some of the local police in Houston go to their home. They told them what he was wanted for and needed to know where he was. His parents were upset but they wanted to make sure that nothing happened to us. The police prayed that they could tap the line, get a call through, and talk to him long enough to get a location. No one was sure if it would work because he knew all of the ends and outs of tapping a line and how long someone needed to be on the phone for them to get a trace. And from the looks of it they had failed.

"What do you want?" Veronica asked. I was still trying to find a way to get us out of this.

"Marcus dead." He said nonchalantly like it was no big deal.

"For what? What have I done to you to make you want to kill me?" I said flabbergasted.

I don't care what anyone said when death is looking you in the face there is no way to keep calm. Things only got worse when I saw him pacing the floor and ranting on and on to no one in particular. All I needed was to be able to get close enough to try and get his gun but he was too far away.

"Because she loved you when she was supposed to love me! Everything I did I did for Adrian but she still wanted you. She gave you her body and a baby and you still don't want her." Keith yelled.

Now he really had me confused. First he was talking about he was mad she wanted me now he's mad because I didn't want her? What kind of Fatal Attraction episode was this?

"I don't want Adrian you can have her." I offered.

"You don't get it do you? SHE DOESN'T WANT ME SHE WANTS YOU!" I've killed innocent people for her and I even risked using my job just to prove my love for her. All I wanted was to be there for her but then she had you baby too!"

"Kadesh doesn't belong to Marcus. He's you baby. Please put the gun down.

Don't make anything worse than it already is. It can be fixed so that you can be with your son." Veronica said. I watched as his eyes softened but then grew cold again.

"Adrian said that was your baby not mine. I asked her and I kept asking her but she said the same thing every time."

"She isn't the most trustworthy person Keith." I said.

"Don't talk about her like that! You don't know her like I do."

"Look over on our dresser and get that piece of paper. It's the DNA test that was done on Kadesh." I told him thinking that maybe if he saw it for himself he would calm down.

We watched him closely and I could have sworn that I heard the alarm chime indicating that someone had opened the garage door. Keith looked up at us smiling still holding the paper.

"He's mine?"

"Yes that is your son. Adrian just told you he wasn't yours because she that if she had then you would stop carrying out the plan. If she made you think that once again Marcus had taken something from you that you would still come after us."

"I can't believe this. Omg I can't believe this." He said stuck in one spot. I was still standing in the place beside the bed when he walked in. I estimated that it was about ten feet or so away from him but I had no clue how to get closer.

Just then I thought I saw a figure in the hallway but I didn't utter a word.

"What are you looking at?" Keith wanted to know as he turned around towards the door and that was all it took in that split second for him to get distracted and I took that opportunity to charge at him.

I heard Veronica scream as we wrestled for the gun and the next think I knew the gun went off and I instantly felt the warm blood start to cover my body.

"MARCUSSSSSSSSSSSSS!"

Chapter Fifteen

Veronica

I had just touched down in Chicago and Mrs. Verna was there waiting on me. I didn't have any luggage because this trip was only for the day and I would be returning home later this evening.

"Hey baby how are you?" she asked embracing me.

"I'm ok. It's just hard to deal with you know?" I told her.

"Let's get going then."

It took us about twenty minutes to get to Mercy University and the closer e got the more nervous I became. This last year has been a living hell for me and I was ready to face my biggest obstacle yet.

Getting out of the car my stomach did a double flip and I felt like I was about to boo boo everywhere. Mrs. Verna signed us in and we sat in the waiting area. A short while later a tall Caucasian doctor came out to sit and talk with us before he let us go back.

"How is she doctor?" Mrs. Verna asked concerned.

"There hasn't been any improvement in her and I'm running out of options. She flips out so much that she constantly has to be sedated and I dint like to keep pumping her full of those meds but I have to for everyone's safety."

"I understand." She said.

"I just want the both of you to understand that she may not know you or even want to talk. So if you see her getting agitated I will advise you to hit the panic button and leave. We aren't sure what she is really capable of." He said getting up so that we could follow behind him.

Walking through the door of Iesha's room and it smelled like pure sulfur. The smell was so overwhelming that I immediately started praying for covering. This room was so full of things that were not of this world and they were letting it be known by the smell they carried.

"Iesha baby it's mommy. I have someone who wants to see you." Her mother said calmly. Iesha was standing in the corner looking at the wall and wouldn't turn around.

"Hey E." I said calling her by her nickname.

This time she turned around. When we made eye contact I felt nothing but pity for her. She was lost and consumed with things that were really out of her control and I felt so bad for her.

Iesha looked me over but didn't say not one word. All she did was turn back around and face the wall again.

"I just came to apologize. I know that some of what you are going through is my fault and if I could do it over I would. I never meant to hurt you and I think that by me leaving the way that I did didn't give you the closure you needed in order to move on and I am truly sorry."

Still no response.

"For once free yourself from all of the pain and turmoil that has taken over your life so that you can heal and move on. You deserve so much better than this. I no longer hold any hatred in my heart for you and I forgive you for every single thing that you did. Now you have to forgive yourself. That's the only way that you will be able to get out of here."

"Baby turn around and talk to her. Let us know what it is that you are feeling. We are listening Iesha." Her mother pleaded.

Slowly she turned around and I saw all of the freshly fallen tears that she had coming down her face. I knew that it wasn't against their policy but I made my way over to her anyway and wrapped my arms around her. The weight of the world was on her shoulders but only she could get rid of that weight with the help of the Lord.

I held her as she broke down or at least that's what I thought she was doing. Before I realized that the sound she was making was laughing instead of crying it was too late. She did some kind of move to get free and tried to come at me and attack me. Iesha was going wild. Screaming and yelling and spitting and going crazy. Mrs. Verna hit the panic button that was located where the doctor told us and not even three seconds later the orderlies were running in the room and subduing her.

"I HOPE YOU ROT IN HELL! JUST LIKE EVERYONE ELSE YOU DIDN'T LOVE ME I WAS JUST THERE! YOU BETTER HOPE I DIE IN HERE BECAUSE IF I DON'T I PROMISE WHEN I GET OUT I. WILL. KILL. YOU!" she screamed as we made our way out of the door.

The ride back to the airport was a silent one. Neither of us knew what to say right away. Before I got out Mrs. Verna finally spoke.

"I'm sorry that you had to go through that at the hand of my child but I admire your strength. I don't know how many people would have been able to endure all that you have to the end. Some would have thrown in the towel long ago. Don't look at today as a failure because the visit didn't go the way that you had planned. It was still victorious because you came out of there a new woman. Forgiveness is the key to unlocking the doors of heaven and I'm thankful that you took that step to let it go.

Please keep her in your prayers because she is going to need all that she can get in order for those demons to be cast out. It may not happen right away but I'm hopeful that it will be done in Jesus' name." she said as she hugged me and cried.

"I owe a lot to you. If it wasn't for you constantly praying for me and telling me to walk away all those years ago I don't know where I would be. But it was the grace of God and the love of Him that you showed me and my family and I can't thank you enough for it all." I said crying tears of my own.

"To God be all the glory sweetheart. Go ahead and go so you don't miss your flight. We will be in touch and please let me know when you get home safely."

"I will. I love you Mrs. Verna."

"I love you too Veronica."

I hugged her once more before getting out and heading inside so that I could finally get back to my regular life.

Epilogue

Veronica

Once I left Chicago from my visit with Iesha I felt a release but I knew there was just one more loose end that I had to tie up before I could close this chapter of my life. It took me a while to decide when I was going to do it so I prayed that when it was time God would let me know.

I walked through the metal detectors and made my way into the visiting room and waited for Adrian to come out. I had no idea what I was going to say to her so I prayed that God would just have his way.

The guard opened the door as the inmates filed in and found their family members that came to visit them. Worry started to set in because the door had closed and Adrian hadn't come in. Just when I was about to leave the door opened up again and in she walked. Now that I was getting a good look at her I could see how stunning she was and how much we resembled one another.

Adrian sat down across from me without saying a word. I didn't know whether or not this would be a reconciling and defining moment in the both of our lives or not but I was willing. Now a few months ago I would have told her to kick rocks and good riddance but I knew that I had to show her the love of God.

"Hey Adrian." I said.

"Hi." Was her simple reply. I could tell she was nervous and so was I but I wanted her to feel comfortable.

"I just came by to say that I was sorry. I hurt you and even though I didn't know that I did you were still hurt by me and I'm sorry."

"How can you be sorry if you did nothing wrong." She asked.

"Because somewhere I dropped the ball. I feel like I could have searched for you or something and maybe we wouldn't be at this point in our lives." I explained.

"I can't let you do that. This was in no way your fault. I've had time to reflect on everything that has happened and I can't let you take the blame for this. I don't even blame our mother and father anymore." She said shocking me.

"I thought you hated Clarence."

"I did. I felt like he loved you more and gave you more but he didn't know about me. How could he love someone that he never knew existed and the same goes for you? Mama did what she thought was best at the time and no matter how I viewed it back then I understand her reasons now. She really didn't have a choice."

"No she didn't. I hate that she was put in a situation where she had to choose like that but what's done is done."

"I thought you had the better life and when I saw you so happy and everything that you had it fueled my anger even more. I wanted you to hurt the way I hurt all of those years."

"But I did hurt Adrian. Daddy wasn't a bad man but he made a ton of bad mistakes that we paid for. In all honestly my life growing up was far from grate but I managed. It wasn't until I left Chicago and started a relationship with God that my life got better. I had to fight some nights just survive the streets but God brought me out of that even while I was in my mess."

"Will you please forgive me?" she asked as she started to cry.

I reached my hand out for hers as I told her, "I already have."

We talked for the remainder of the two hour visit about everything from our favorite colors to what we liked to eat. It was so good to be sitting there talking to the sister that I always wanted and finding out that we had so much in common with one another. I even told her about God and expressed how important it was to have a relationship with Him and by the time I left she had repented for all of her sins and gave her life to Christ.

******

"Come on girls we are going to be late for church. You know that after service we have to get right to the airport so we can head out for our cruise tomorrow." I yelled up the stairs. I don't care how early I got them up they were never on time.

"Here we come!" Dynasty yelled back.

I was finally back in a happy place and I know that it was all because of God. We couldn't have made it without Him. Some days the memories still got to me but not as bad now as before. I chose to move out of the house we were living in because it was just too painful every time I went into the bedroom Marcus and I once shared. No matter who hard I tried I couldn't get that blood stain out of the carpet and the smell still lingered in the air. I cried as soon as I would get through the door until one day I couldn't take it any longer.

    Piling up in the car we headed towards our church. It was so good to be back in the house of the Lord and to see so many of our members continue to support us. They helped us more than they realized.

As we were getting out Torre, Malachi, Lailani, and my little butterball Cadence pulled up right beside us. Once they unstrapped her little fat self she hauled tail over to where I was. Scooping her up in my arms I littered her face with lots of kisses as she giggled. I tried putting her down but instead she drew her legs up so that her feet couldn't touch the ground. I laughed at her as I saw her trying to stretch behind me.

"Come to Papa my angel." Marcus said getting out of the driver's seat.

He grabbed her as she put her small arms around his neck as tight as she could and put her head on his shoulders. I looked at him and silently thanked God that it was not him that had gotten shot that night Keith came to our house.

When the gun went off we thought it was from Keith's gun and the tussling he and Marcus were doing but instead it was from Detective Ramos. The reason it looked like Marcus wasn't moving because he had the wind knocked out of him when they fell and Keith landed on him.

Unfortunately Keith didn't survive the incident. Detective Ramos let us know that his father had finally gotten through on the phone and was able to keep him on the line long enough to get a trace. He told us that a few days before Keith broke into the house he had caught him driving real slow down the street. It was slow enough for him to get the license plate number off of the car that registered to an address in Houston,

Texas. Once they sent local officers there they discovered the address belonged to Keith's parents. From then on it made it easier to track him. Had they not gotten there when they did who knows what would have happened.

"Come on yall before we are late." Marcus said as Destiny grabbed Christian and I got little Kadesh out of his car seat.

Yes he was still with us. There was no way that I could let my nephew grow up without anyone to take care of him. His mother was locked away for God knows how long and his father was dead. Marcus and I decided to just raise him as our own and once he was older and if Adrian wanted to we would sit him down and explain it all. The last thing that we wanted was for him to have to deal with anything that Adrian and I had to from being kept in the dark.

"Hold on wait on me. You know my knees bad." I heard my mother say.

If someone had told me that I would have the relationship that I had now with my mother years ago I would call them crazy. But the bond we had created was like no other. She had even found her a nice little house a few blocks over so that she could be close to us and Marcus and I paid for it. Anything she needed we made sure to get her and in return her spot was the hot spot for the grandkids when Marcus and I needed Mommy and Daddy time.

    As a family we were all thankful for the challenges we had face but we were excited now for everything that the future held in store. I was a confessing First Lady

but in the end I was able to take it all back.

THE END!

Discussion Questions

1. From the very beginning how did you all view Veronica?

2. Do you think that Marcus represented a true man of God well?

3. I know the Millhouse children weren't the main focus of the story but how do you thing they were portrayed?

4. Did Iesha and Adrian deserve to be forgiven? Why or why not?

5. Why do you think that most church people love to knock leaders down once their flaws are revealed?

6. How do you feel about Keith and the role he played?

7. Were the actions of Veronica justified towards Marcus? Towards Kadesh? Why or why not?

8. Do you think that Sarita had any other options other than leaving Veronica behind? Would you have made the same choice?

9. Which character do you relate to the most and why?

10. If this series was turned into a movie how likely is it that you would go to see it?

Thank you all so much again for riding with me through this series and getting all up in the First Lady's business! Be on the lookout for more from me!

Other Titles By Denora

God Doesn't Make Mistakes

God Doesn't Break Promises

God Doesn't Make Mistakes: Josephine's Revelations

Confessions of a First Lady

Confessions of a First Lady 2

The Pastor's Other Woman

The Pastor's Other Woman 2 (Coming Soon)

Thuggin' At The Altar

He Loved The Hell Out Of Me: A Kingdom Anthology

Made in the USA
Lexington, KY
14 June 2016